D0768948

The Ghost Squad Flies Concorde

By the Same Author

The Ghost Squad Breaks Through

The Ghost Squad Flies Concorde

by E. W. Hildick

A Ghost Squad Book

E. P. DUTTON   NEW YORK

CREEKSIDE ELEMENTARY SCHOOL
MORENO VALLEY UNIFIED SCHOOL DISTRICT

To the memory of my mother,
EDITH ALICE HILDICK,
who warned me about
the whole shebang

Copyright © 1985 by E. W. Hildick

All rights reserved. No part of this publication may be reproduced or transmitted in any form or by any means, electronic or mechanical, including photocopy, recording, or any information storage and retrieval system now known or to be invented, without permission in writing from the publisher, except by a reviewer who wishes to quote brief passages in connection with a review written for inclusion in a magazine, newspaper, or broadcast.

LIBRARY OF CONGRESS CATALOGING IN PUBLICATION DATA

Hildick, E. W. (Edmund Wallace), date.
  The Ghost Squad flies Concorde.

  (A Ghost Squad book)
  Summary: Four young ghosts who have banded together to prevent crimes fly to England to investigate a swindler.
  [1. Ghosts—Fiction. 2. England—Fiction.
3. Mystery and detective stories] I. Title.
II. Series: Hildick, E. W. (Edmund Wallace), date.
Ghost Squad book.
PZ7.H5463Gho 1985 [Fic] 85-1487
ISBN 0-525-44191-3

Published in the United States by E. P. Dutton,
2 Park Avenue, New York, N.Y. 10016

Published simultaneously in Canada by
Fitzhenry & Whiteside Limited, Toronto

Editor: Julie Amper

Printed in the U.S.A.   COBE   First Edition
10 9 8 7 6 5 4 3 2 1

Contents

1
Strange Guests

There was something wrong about those two kids. Something very wrong indeed. And what might have made the boys' presence seem even more disturbing was the fact that almost everything else was going quietly and smoothly in the elegant Lakeview Hotel restaurant that lunchtime.

Outside, the hot July sunlight was beating down on the lake and breaking up, shimmering, on its surface. But inside the restaurant it was cool, and even though most of the customers had chosen tables by the windows, their eyes were protected from the dazzle by the delicately tinted plate glass. The double thickness of that glass also protected their ears from the racket outdoors: the rasp of speedboats and the clamor of raised voices and radios at the nearby picnic area.

Except for the two boys, the only thing that threatened to spoil the atmosphere inside that restaurant was the laughter of a woman sitting at a table in a far corner. Every so often it kept breaking out—a harsh, coarse barking. It made the other customers lift their eyebrows and made some of the waiters wince. The man with her seemed to be aware of the embarrassment. Whenever the laughter looked like it was going on too long, he was always quick to change the subject and get her to be serious and quiet down.

But he did nothing about those two boys. Neither he nor anyone else seemed to be embarrassed by them, even though they were far more out of place than any burst of raucous laughter. And yet they were standing right there, hovering over the man and woman, only inches away, listening to every word they said.

It wasn't as if they were junior waiters, either. They weren't dressed for the job. *They* didn't wear short spotless white jackets and neatly pressed black trousers. In fact they weren't dressed for that restaurant at all—either as helpers or customers.

One—the older of the two, a pale anxious-looking kid of about fourteen—wasn't properly dressed for any place that hot July. He was wearing a thick, black imitation-leather windbreaker, tightly zippered, with the collar stuck up around his ears. And as if that wasn't warm enough for him, he was also wearing a red nylon scarf.

The other kid had a much more carefree look. He was suitably dressed for the weather, if not for the Lakeview Hotel restaurant. He had on a pair of light, faded blue jeans and a thin yellow T-shirt. There was a logo on the T-shirt—a wheel of letters and numbers at the end of spokes, with a big letter *G* where the hub should have been. But it would have been difficult for anyone to spell out or even count those smaller letters and numbers, because he was never still for more than a second at a time.

Like right now, for instance.

While the older one just stood there, staring with a worried frown at the woman, the thirteen-year-old kept darting around the table, bending to read the wine list or to inspect the food with his sharp brown eyes or to bring his head so close to the man's wrist that his shaggy black hair was in danger of brushing the lamb chops on the plate.

"For Pete's sake, keep still, Carlos!" said the older boy.

"Hey! Wow! It is, Danny! It is!" said Carlos, straightening up, his eyes sparkling. "That watch he's wearing is a real Rolex Oyster! Solid gold!"

His voice yelped with excitement. It too had a barking quality, in his case like that of a young sheepdog. But no eyebrows were raised at the other end of the room. No waiters winced.

Even the couple at the table paid no attention. Even when Carlos dipped his head again to make quite sure the watch really was made of gold, at the same split second the man glanced at it himself. Even when Carlos's shaggy head came between the man's eyes and the watch face. Even then, there was no comment from the man.

Which was strange, because although he was well dressed and quietly spoken—and although he was smiling at the woman and doing his best to make a good impression on her—he didn't look like the sort of guy who'd be pestered by a kid. There were some hard lines in the pudgy flesh around his small smirking mouth. And the eyes, under the carefully thinned eyebrows, and the soft furlike fuzz of sandy hair—such soft and babylike hair that it looked too good to be true—those eyes were as cold as a snake's.

"You sure you wouldn't like some more wine, Veronica?" he said, in a voice like sifted sugar.

He reached out with the bottle.

"Not *yet*, Rick!" The woman clapped a hand over her half-emptied glass, nearly upsetting it. She giggled. "What are you trying to do? Get me drunk *this* early in the day?"

"That wouldn't be so unusual!" said Danny.

The words came out in a loud groaning tone. But the couple didn't pay the slightest attention. Only the other kid looked up sharply and said:

"Hey, come on, Danny! You can't always be following your mother around, worrying like this. You'll—heh! heh!—you'll be worrying yourself to death!"

Even Danny smiled faintly at that crack.

After all, it was rather funny, considering . . .

Considering that both he and Carlos were ghosts!

2
The London Call

Yes. Danny Green and Carlos Gomez were ghosts.

That was why no one else in the room could see or hear them. They were sealed off from the living people in there even more tightly than those people were sealed off from the blare and glare of the outside world. The two boys could see each other, hear each other, even touch each other and make themselves felt by each other. In their own eyes, they were just as solid as the living persons present.

But it didn't work in reverse—except in very special circumstances.

"No, but this really worries me," said Danny. "I mean, it's obvious! The guy's just after her money!"

Carlos said nothing. It sure looked that way, he thought. After all, Mrs. Green was no pinup. Even her new lilac silk suit couldn't disguise the bulky sprawl of her figure. An expensive hairdo and golden-highlights dye job did something for her face, all right—but so far she'd found no beautician to fix the sagging jawline or repair the hands, with their bitten fingernails and the roughness caused by her former job as a scrubwoman. As for the nicotine stains, it looked as if only plastic surgery would ever get rid of them.

The man, though, was quite handsome, in a slimy sort of way.

"I still can't believe my luck," he said, with a sugary sigh. He took another glance at his watch before gazing into her eyes again. "Meeting up with you after all these years."

Mrs. Green simpered. Then, just as if she *had* heard the words of her dead son, she said:

"Oh, come on, Rick! You're just saying all this. You're just after my money, is all."

She knocked back the rest of the wine and pushed the empty glass toward him.

"No," he said, refilling it. "No way. Listen . . ." He chuckled, and the sound was like thin maple syrup being poured onto a tin plate. "How many more times do I have to say this? When I was a kid, I was crazy about you. I mean it. But you were two grades ahead, and, well, to a kid, that's like a whole generation."

He sighed.

Mrs. Green's eyes were filling up.

"Aw! Go on!" she murmured.

"Mother!" groaned Danny.

"It's true," said the man.

He brushed the back of a soft, golden brown, hair-

6

less hand across his eyes. Not that there was any moisture *there*. Those eyes were still as hard and dry as a snake's.

"And even when I left town for good," he continued, "I still kept on thinking of you. Even when I left the country. All those years. All those places. And now, when I come back and find you—a widow with four kids and still looking great—"

"It used to be five kids," moaned Mrs. Green, the tears really beginning to roll now.

"Yeah, yeah!" he said softly, reaching out to pat her hand. "There was Danny—"

"He was a fine, lovely boy!" wailed Mrs. Green. "So good. He worked s-so hard. Wh-when we were poor—"

"Which is why your lawyer is quite right to go after those factory owners for all that compensation money," said the man, gripping her hand. "They *deserve* to be— to be forced to cough up."

Mrs. Green wasn't to be consoled that easily.

"I'd give it all up," she said, in a low voice, "if only Danny would come back to life."

Danny felt a lump rise in his throat. His mother really meant that, he could tell. Even Carlos was looking touched.

"Sure! Sure you would!" said the man, returning to his food. "More wine?"

Mrs. Green didn't seem to hear.

"Sometimes," she murmured, glancing around, "sometimes I feel he's still not far away."

"Of course," said the man. He munched on a tender morsel of lamb. "It's only natural. Human relations.

7

They count for much more than that. Even two hundred thousand dollars is nothing compared to that."

"Two million," said Mrs. Green. She braced herself and took another swig. "Two million. That's what the lawyer thinks we'll get in the end."

"Two million then. *If* everything goes OK. But what I'm saying, Veronica, is this. It's just peanuts as far as I'm concerned. My business in London brings me twice that much in a good year. So why should I—?"

"So you say."

"Huh?"

Mrs. Green was smiling again—coyly, craftily.

"That's what you *say* you earn, Rick."

He sat back. It was as if he'd been waiting for this.

"And I can *prove* it," he said. "Here, take a look."

He reached into an inside pocket and pulled out a small brochure.

"That's a picture of the business premises. Slap-bang in the center of Hampstead, London. A prime site in the antiques trade, I can tell you!"

Mrs. Green bent over it. So did Carlos.

"Well, that's your name over the window, all right," said the woman.

"Richard Jackman, Sole Proprietor," Carlos read out.

Danny hadn't even bothered to look. He was still staring at the man with deep distrust.

"And the address *is* Hampstead, sure enough," said Carlos as Mrs. Green turned the page. "It looks OK to me."

"Yeah!" said Danny. "And to Mom, too. But who's to say—"

8

As if anticipating the next question, the man tossed another document across the table.

"And there's the latest deposit account statement from my bank in London."

Both Mrs. Green and Carlos stared at the figures with widening eyes.

"Wow!" yelped Carlos.

"Hmm!" murmured Mrs. Green.

"And that's only part of my investments, of course," said the man.

"Funny name for a bank," murmured Mrs. Green.

"One of the oldest and best in London," said Mr. Jackman. He took another glance at his watch. "The Queen of England banks there, too."

"Really?" Mrs. Green giggled. "She stands in line waiting to cash *her* checks? Haw! Haw!"

The waiter approaching the table winced.

"Take it easy, Veronica!" murmured Mr. Jackman.

But the waiter hadn't come with a complaint.

"A phone call from London, sir," he said.

Again Jackman glanced at his watch.

"That'll be my associate," he said. "Tell him to hang up and I'll get back to him in a few minutes."

He turned to Mrs. Green.

"Look, I'd better take it soon. It's a big business deal we have cooking. That's why I want to call him back from my room. More private. You want to come along, Veronica?"

Mrs. Green shook her head, with that coy grin on her face.

"Huh-uh! *You* want to get us a bad name?"

Jackman smirked.

"You think this is a trick, don't you? Just to get you alone, you wicked girl!"

"I'm going to puke!" said Danny.

"Anyway," said Jackman, getting up. "It really is important business. But it won't take more than two or three minutes."

"Go right ahead," said Mrs. Green, reaching for the bottle. "I'll be just fine here."

"I bet she was right, though," said Danny, watching the man leave. "Just a trick. I bet the call was from some buddy of his in a local pool hall. London!"

But Carlos couldn't leave it at that.

"Why don't we check and put your mind at rest?" he said, plucking Danny's sleeve. "Let's follow him and see what happens."

"Why not?" said Danny, but without much enthusiasm.

"So let's *move!*" said Carlos. "It'll be no use getting there after he's closed the door to his room."

Thus reminded of one of the major disadvantages of being a ghost, Danny moved.

3
A Case for the Full Ghost Squad

Anyone who thinks ghosts are able to walk through walls and other solid objects can forget it. Ghosts who've been foolish enough or raw enough to try it have found that strange things are liable to happen in such cases.

Both Danny and Carlos knew this. Which is why they hastened to catch up with Jackman and stay with him along the corridor leading to the guest rooms. And that was why they stuck *very* close to his side as, whistling softly to himself, he unlocked the door to his room and went in.

"Nice room!" said Carlos, immediately beginning to prowl around.

"Now we'll see," muttered Danny, interested only in the phone on the night table and who the man would call.

Jackman's first move was to sit on the edge of the bed and take a plastic card from his wallet.

"Phone company credit card," said Carlos, giving it a glance in passing.

Jackman's next act was to pick up the phone book and flip through the front pages.

"Oh, he's going to call London all right!" said Carlos, darting back to look over the man's shoulder, as Jackman left the book open at the page headed International Calling. "The trouble with you, Danny, is you worry too much. Too suspicious."

"We'll see," grunted Danny.

The man was now scribbling some figures on a scratch pad.

"*Zero-one*," said Carlos. "That's the Calling Card operator. . . . Now he's adding *forty-four*—that's the United Kingdom. And *one*—that'll be"—he bent over the book—"yeah—London."

"Sure," said Danny. "But who's to say *who* he's—"

"Sh!" Carlos gripped his arm. "I'll tell you in a second."

The man was almost through dialing the five numbers he'd jotted down. Now he was continuing to dial the actual London number he wanted. Carlos was watching every twist of Jackman's finger.

"Well *that's* true enough, too!" said Carlos, when the man sat back, listening. "He's just dialed the number on the antique-store leaflet thing he was showing your mother."

"You sure?"

"Sure!" said Carlos, as the man read out his credit card number to the operator. "I never forget a number. Numbers and me are like peanut butter and jelly. I—"

"Be quiet!" said Danny. "It's ringing at the other end."

12

The ringing tone had sounded very clear, even from where they were standing. But both boys instinctively moved their heads closer as a piping voice—male, British—said, "Hello! That you, Jackman?"

"Yeah," said Jackman. "It's me. What's the matter, Fred? Think I'd run out on you or something?"

"Of course not! Not that you wouldn't like to, I bet. But you know that wouldn't be wise, don't you, Jackman?"

The voice sounded impatient and menacing—but also very nervous.

Jackman smiled.

"Is that all you wanted to say, Fred? I mean do you want to know about the business I came for, or not?"

"Business! Buried treasure! If you think you could fool me with that load of baloney, you're—"

"Hey, hey, hey! Easy, Fred! That buried treasure business is no baloney, believe me!" Jackman glanced at a pile of old books and pamphlets on the dressing table. "As soon as I get over my jet lag, I'm going to get down to some serious exploration. But in the meantime you'll be glad to know I've stumbled into another possible deal. More regular. More your kind."

"Oh?"

The voice sounded calmer.

"Yeah. Old school friend of mine. Very charming lady now. Lots of—uh—liquid capital."

Danny stiffened. Carlos gripped his arm. The voice at the other end said cautiously, "Oh? Oh, yes? Is this another of your jokes, Jackman?"

"Do I ever joke about women, Fred? Especially rich ones. No. Seriously. She's a widow. Just come into money—which is nice."

The way Jackman said those last three words—drawling them, even slightly lisping them—made it very plain just *whom* he thought it was nice for.

"Yeah," he went on, "one of her kids got killed in an accident—"

The man at the other end made a strange noise—part groan, part howl—and mumbled something that neither boy managed to catch.

"No!" said Jackman. "*Months* before I arrived. Look, man—what are you trying to say?"

Now it was Jackman who sounded menacing. The other seemed to shrink a little, judging from his tone.

"Nothing. Sorry, Rick." Then the tone stiffened. "I suppose I was thinking of Mrs. Cramer and *her* kids."

Jackman scowled.

"Well, don't! Don't think. You're not paid to think. You're paid to keep your trap shut, my friend. And to mind the store. *I* do the thinking. OK?"

"Certainly. Of course. I was only—"

"Like I was saying. This lady is going to be very well-off. Damages. Compensation money for the kid's death. Which occurred *months* ago, Fred. *Months*. When part of an old burned-out factory he was exploring fell on him."

"Oh, I see," said the other man, sounding sympathetic.

"Yeah!" sneered Jackman, sounding quite the opposite. "Isn't it tragic!" Carlos glanced anxiously at Danny. But Danny was concentrating on Jackman's next words. "Her lawyer's a real sharpie. He has the factory owners over a barrel. He had them begging to settle out of court right from Day One. He's managed to gouge quite a bundle out of them already. Probably doing a side deal with them, but she's too dumb to see that. Of course, whatever she ends up with, she'll blow it all inside a year." Then Jackman's small mouth widened into a repulsive leer as he gave his syrupy chuckle again. "Without a good man at her side to advise her and take care of her investments!"

"You—you're not thinking of *marrying* her, Jackman?"

"Well"—the leer shrank as Jackman made a wry face—"well, sure! If I have to. It won't be the first time, as you well know."

"Yes. Well. The sooner you come up with *something*, the better, I suppose. Things are getting very tight at this end. And—and—well, quite frankly—there's the Other matter. I—I . . ."

Jackman sniggered.

"Oh-oh! Don't tell me you've been *seeing* things again, Fred? Not the *ghosts* again!"

Danny and Carlos frowned.

"As a matter of fact, yes. Last night. In my sleep. But so *real*, Rick! So—"

"Dreams, man. That's all."

"Maybe. But so vivid. And always the kids. Both of them. Just like when they were alive. And—and they always say the same things. About how—how—well, *you* know."

Jackman shook his head slowly.

"I know. You need a break, Fred. Change of scene. Anyway, I'd better go now. I'll get back to you later this week. OK?"

Before returning to Mrs. Green, Jackman went into the bathroom.

"I wonder what *that* was all about?" said Carlos, while they were waiting. "The ghosts. I mean *you* know and *I* know that ghosts can't show themselves to living people. Except in very special—"

"Never mind that now," said Danny. "It was probably the guy's nerves, like Jackman said. What worries me is what he was saying about this other woman and her kids in connection with *me* being killed."

"Yeah!" grunted Carlos. He had resumed his prowling and was now peering at the pile of old books. The top one was in fact more like a leather box made to look like a book. It was stained and frayed and had a brass clasp. There were two labels on the lid: one old and yellow but neatly inscribed; the other new and carelessly stuck on. The latter said: *LOT 165. Sold to R. Jackman, Hampstead.* The former said, in fine, flourishing, faded handwriting, with the *s*'s formed like *f*'s: *Colonel H. P. Halliday. His Private Papers.*

Carlos's fingers itched to lift the lid. But that, for a ghost, was quite impossible. He turned to Danny.

"Whatever happened to that other woman and her kids obviously happened over in England. There's nothing we can do about that."

"I guess not," said Danny. "But—well—it sounds bad for Mom and *her* kids. Maybe we'd better talk it over with the others. Maybe—look out! Here he comes."

As they slipped out of the room with Jackman, Carlos nodded.

"Yeah, you're right, Danny. This is beginning to sound *very* suspicious. It's definitely a case for the full Ghost Squad."

16

4
The Ghost Squad

The full Ghost Squad consisted of six members: four ghosts and two living persons.

Danny Green had been a ghost for about five months.

Carlos Gomez had been a ghost for a little over a year. He had died at the age of thirteen, and so, as a ghost, that was the age he would always remain in the eyes of himself and other ghosts.

This had seemed strange to Danny at first, because when they were both alive, he and Carlos had been roughly the same age. But Danny had lived to be fourteen. Therefore that was how *he'd* always be as a ghost—one year older than Carlos.

He'd soon grown used to this, but Danny sometimes found his head beginning to swim when he thought about the people still alive.

"I mean, if I hang around as a ghost long enough I'll see my kid brothers and sisters grow older than *me!*"

"Don't worry," Joe Armstrong had told him. "Ghosts very rarely stay around for more than a couple of years. Just long enough to do what they feel they *must* do. Then . . ."

"Then what?"

Joe had shrugged.

"They just vanish. Go to another level of existence. I guess."

Joe was the leader of the Ghost Squad and knew more about the facts of afterlife. He'd been a ghost for over eighteen months. He'd been twenty-three at the time of death, and that, of course, was how he remained in ghosthood: a husky six-footer with broad shoulders, red hair and a pleasant chunky face. He always wore a gray T-shirt with the words ARMSTRONG CONSTRUCTION stenciled across the chest. He'd been the owner of a small construction company by the time he was twenty-one, and he was still proud of the fact.

Karen Hansen, the fourth ghost, was second to Joe in seniority as far as age went. She'd been sixteen at the time of death and, like Joe, looked a picture of health. Her deep tan was set off beautifully by her long blond hair and the clothes she wore: a thin red shirt and white shorts.

"But you still rank after me in length of ghosthood," Carlos used to say, laughing shyly at this girl he used to look up to as a school beauty when they were both alive. "Don't you forget that!"

This was true. Karen had been killed a few months after Carlos's death.

"That's OK, Carlos," she would reply. "I won't."

And there was something shy in her smile, too, when she said this. Because young Carlos had more to justify his claim than a mere few months' start on her as a ghost.

Without Carlos and his scientific genius, the ghosts would never have made the big breakthrough that enabled them to communicate with the living.

In fact, it had been Carlos's scientific genius that had killed him. He'd been working on making special modifications to the word processor he'd designed and built with his friend Wacko Williams when he gripped the wrong part of the chassis with one hand and started tugging at the wrong lead with the other. And that was the end of Carlos as a living person.

"A most unfortunate accident," the medical examiner had said.

"A brilliant scientific career nipped in the bud," the principal had told the assembled school.

"He was always so darned *careless!*" Wacko had said, through his tears. "He'd get so excited about the wild discoveries he was making, he'd forget the simple safety rules."

Sudden violent death was one thing all four ghosts had in common. Besides Carlos's electrocution and Danny's crushing under tons of bricks, Karen's and Joe's had been just as horrible—Karen's under the wheels of a tractor-trailer truck, and Joe's from a fall from the tenth story of a half-finished building.

Another thing they—and most other ghosts—had

in common was their undamaged looks and unspoiled clothing. The clothes were the ones they'd felt best in around the time of death. And no matter how badly torn and messed up those clothes had been as a result of the accidents, and no matter how badly mangled their living bodies had been, in ghosthood they survived intact. To themselves and each other, the ghosts looked just as they had before the dreadful events had occurred.

And there was one other, very special thing the four had in common.

Like most ghosts—*most*, not *all*—they had stayed around on earth because they were abnormally concerned about their relatives or friends.

Danny was worried about his kid brothers and sisters, who'd depended on him so much while he was alive.

Karen was anxious about her father, who wrongly blamed himself for her death, just because she'd been running an errand for him at the time.

Joe was concerned because his young wife had had a nervous breakdown thinking he might—just might—have committed suicide.

"Which was a bunch of baloney!" Joe would say fiercely. "Suicides *never* come back, *never* hang around as ghosts. They just disappear. Totally."

Besides, Joe knew very well that he'd been pushed off that building. By whom, though, was still a mystery—even to him.

"But I'll solve it one of these days. You'll see!"

Carlos was, as a ghost, just as he'd been in life: an exceptional case. Being a loving son and brother, he'd been terribly worried about his family's shock and grief at first. But the Gomez family was a healthy, outgoing bunch. There'd never been any danger of any of them not getting over his death, given time.

Being a genius, however, was something else. It meant that not even death had been able to pull him away from the work he'd been so passionately involved in. That was how the breakthrough had come to be made.

The other three had been delighted when Carlos first demonstrated his ability to communicate with the living. It seemed like they would finally be able to comfort their relatives.

But there was a snag.

The only living people they could communicate with were Wacko Williams and Danny's friend, Buzz Phillips.

"And even if we went to your folks with a message direct from you," Buzz said to the ghosts, "do you think they'd *believe* us?"

"No way," Wacko had said, glumly. "They'd think we'd gone bananas or something."

So while they were wondering if and how they'd ever get around this snag, the idea of the Ghost Squad had been born.

"Because that's one thing we *can* do," Joe had declared. "We *can* fight the crimes we see going on all around us. Especially when they threaten to harm any of the folks we care about. With Buzz and Wacko as our assistants and messengers, we can surely get word to the police in time to prevent those crimes."

Well, even that hadn't been as easy as it had

sounded. And Buzz and Wacko soon proved themselves to be more important than mere messengers or assistants. Before the very first case was as much as a day old, the two living boys had graduated as full members.

Wacko Williams was a thin, nervous black kid of fifteen. He'd been Carlos's best friend. Wacko's parents were very well-off, and they'd always encouraged him in his hobbies and pursuits. Since he was an electronics buff like Carlos, this meant that his bedroom-den had soon become more and more like a research laboratory—dominated by the word processor in the middle of the long table under the window. Even Carlos's death hadn't put more than a temporary crimp in Wacko's enthusiasm.

"I kind of feel I owe it to Carlos's memory to go on with his experiments, Mom," he had said, shortly afterward.

"Well just *you* be careful is all!" had been Mrs. Williams's only comment.

The other living member, Buzz Phillips, had been drafted when Wacko had found it too difficult to cope on his own. Buzz was fourteen and had been with Danny in the old factory when Danny was killed. Thanks to Danny's last-second shove, Buzz had escaped unharmed.

Taller than Wacko, and much more athletic, he was generally less jittery, less likely to panic or despair. Only once, at the very beginning, had the smile trembled at the corners of his wide, good-humored mouth and something like real fear crept into his deep-set brown eyes. That was when Wacko had broken the news to him.

"It wasn't the idea of *ghosts* that scared me," he admitted later. "I just thought you'd gone completely crazy, and I was wondering when you were going to try and beat my brains out with a soldering iron or something!"

These, then, were the six individuals who gathered in Wacko's bedroom that July afternoon at 3:30. The two living boys could see and hear only themselves. The four ghosts could see and hear themselves *and* the living boys.

But right then, at the start of the meeting, no one was looking at any of the others. All eyes were on the word processor, switched on, with its screen faintly glowing.

"All set, Carlos?" said Joe.

Carlos nodded, without turning his head away from the word processor. He was standing directly in front of it. Buzz and Wacko were sitting on straight-backed chairs, on either side of him. The rest of the squad stood a little way back.

"OK, then," said Joe. "Tell them we're all here and what the new case is all about."

Then Carlos raised his shoulders slightly, gave them a loosening shake and began his amazing performance.

5
Strategy

Amazing was the word for that performance, all right!

Even the ghosts, who'd seen it many times before, couldn't help holding their breath.

Sure, they knew that Carlos was familiar with every microchip and circuit in that machine—every *bit, byte, gate* and *bus* (to use some of the terms he and Wacko were so fond of kicking around). And sure, they knew that Carlos had hit on a way of directing the micro-micro-micro-energy that every ghost possesses into those circuits without even touching the keys.

They even suspected (Danny did, anyway) that maybe it wasn't strictly necessary for Carlos to stab with his fingers the way he did, over the keyboard, without actually touching it, as if he were typing in thin air. Stabbing and swaying and staring pop-eyed like an old-time carnival hypnotist.

"Just an extra helping of the Gomez pizzazz," was Danny's opinion.

But, pizzazz or no pizzazz, Carlos could *do* it. He could activate those circuits the way some ghosts could get small swarming insects to cluster around them, or induce floating particles of mist to form into definite shapes, or give objects that were finely balanced the last micro-micro-micro-shove that caused pictures to fall from loose hooks or glasses to fall from the edges of shelves—things that made living witnesses start talking about "poltergeists."

Carlos could do it with that machine, making it say on the screen whatever he wanted it to say. But it still seemed like a miracle to the others. A miracle that might fail him at any time, come the slightest lapse of confidence. Just the way a ball player's arm might fail *him*. Or a trapeze artiste's timing.

Which is why the ghosts were watching him now in an agony of suspense, wondering if *this* might turn out to be one of those times.

It was the same with Buzz and Wacko. They'd never actually *seen* the ghost of Carlos at work. But they'd certainly witnessed the results. And they too were in suspense, wondering if this might be the day something went wrong.

Buzz's eyes were narrowed to slits as he stared at the screen and chewed a corner of his bottom lip. The sweat was starting up on Wacko's forehead. . . .

Well, Carlos didn't keep them in suspense long. It only seemed long—the two or three seconds' pause as he lifted his fingers into position and accelerated the swaying of his shoulders before starting to stab the air.

Then the screen began to flicker, and the following words were formed:

"Ghost Squad all present. Details of new case to follow. Please pay close attention."

The witnesses—ghosts and living alike—all let out their breath in long, deep sighs.

Carlos's words on the screen always started with that same stiff formality. But it wasn't long before they began to read the way he spoke: nervously, enthusiastically, in sentences that were sometimes long and singing, sometimes short and crackling.

"So there was this guy in there with Danny's mother, and, boy, was he laying it on her, bragging about how much he had in the bank, which maybe was true or maybe he'd faked the statement, who knows. . . ."

And later:

"And that was it. It. It-it-it. Right then we knew. The guy was crooked. And dangerous. With Danny's mom and the kids next in line!"

In this way, Carlos completed his report. Then, after adding some more, concerning what Joe and Karen had already had to say about it, he became very formal again.

"So now we would greatly appreciate your own comments and/or queries. Thank you for your attention and over to you."

Wacko and Buzz didn't have to operate the machine. They knew the others would hear them. So they simply turned their heads to where they thought the ghosts would be standing.

"Well—" Buzz began. He glanced at Wacko. "If it's OK with you, Wacko?"

"Sure. Go ahead. You're probably going to say what I'm thinking anyway."

"OK. So the obvious thing to do is warn Mrs. Green somehow. Right?"

Buzz and Wacko turned back to the screen.

"Right," the message flickered back. *"But how? I mean, we've been through this before."*

"You mean Mrs. Green would never believe us, don't you?" said Wacko, gloomily. "She'd want to know how come we were so sure about this guy. And what could we say to *that?*"

"Affirmative," said the screen. *"That is our opinion too."*

"And you can tell them this also," Karen said to Carlos. "Tell them that if Mrs. Green is as charmed by the man as all that, she won't *want* to believe he's a crook."

As Carlos transmitted Karen's comment, the two living boys nodded.

"So now tell them this," said Joe. "The only thing we *can* do is concentrate on the guy's criminal activities. Find out what he's really up to. And what he's done already. Then let the police know."

"Sure," said Carlos, turning from the machine with a frown, "but I've been thinking about that myself. And all right—so we can follow the guy around easily enough. But by the time we catch him in a criminal act, it could be too late for Mrs. Green. . . . Uh—sorry, Danny! But that's the way it could be."

"I know," said Danny, his shoulders slumping a little. "And too late for the kids, too. I just can't forget what the other guy was saying about those other kids, in London."

Karen sighed.

"Yes. It's a shame we can't dig into that. Over there—where"—she shuddered slightly—"whatever the crime *was*, it's been committed already. But that would mean going to London."

Joe was starting to say something when Wacko interrupted.

"Hey, you guys! You gone to sleep or something? Share with us, why don't you?"

"*Sorry!*" the screen apologized. "*We got carried away. We were saying . . .*"

So Carlos brought them up to date.

Buzz nodded when Karen's comment was screened.

"Yeah. That *is* a shame. I guess we'll just have to make do with what you can find out over here."

"And hope it'll be enough—and in time," added Wacko.

But the ghosts weren't listening. With a big grin on his face, Joe was already putting forward his proposition.

"Well, why *don't* we go to London? As ghosts, we're always taking free rides in cars around town. Why don't we take a free ride on a *plane?*"

Karen's eyes sparkled.

"Of course! Why not? All we need do is take the town limo to Kennedy Airport."

"Fellas!" came Wacko's pleading voice. "We can't *hear* you. Remember? The picture. Please put us in it."

When Carlos had apologized again and done as Wacko had requested, both living boys brightened up.

"Now you're talking!" said Buzz.

"Hey!" said Wacko. "The Ghost Squad goes international!" Then his face clouded. "Or some of it does, anyway."

"*How's that?*" flashed the message on the screen.

"Well, *you* can't go, for one, Carlos," said Wacko. "I mean *we* need you *here*. You're the only one of the ghosts who can work the machine."

"And one of you will have to stay and keep an eye on Jackman," said Buzz. "A really *close* eye. Night and day. Neither of *us* could do that."

Carlos's face was a study. A look of sheer outrage had leaped into his eyes, and his mouth had opened wide in protest. But no words came out, as the good sense of what Wacko had said got through to him.

Joe looked at him anxiously. He seemed to be wondering if Carlos's disappointment might not upset his skill with the machine.

"Take it easy, Carlos," he said. "Maybe—"

"But you might *need* me over there," Carlos said. "Such a long way. Air travel. All *kinds* of technical problems might arise. We—we may need to communicate with a living person over there. With the *police* over there. With *Scotland Yard* over there. You may need my electronics know-how."

He spoke fast, but without much conviction. He knew—and he knew the others would know, when they thought about it—that nobody in London, not even at Scotland Yard, was likely to have an exact duplicate of that word processor on the table. Hadn't he practically built it himself?

Joe humored him.

"OK! OK! Calm down, Carlos. You wouldn't be

the best one to stay behind and follow developments with the Green family anyway."

Danny coughed.

"No. Gee! I guess I'm the guy for that job, really. But—"

"No! *Not* really!" Joe sounded very positive. "In my opinion, you're the last one for that job. You're too close to the—uh—potential victims. You'd be getting too uptight."

"Why don't we see what Buzz and Wacko think?" Karen reminded them, having caught the look of impatience on the faces of the living boys.

Two minutes later, she wished she'd kept her mouth shut.

"It seems to me," said Buzz, "that Karen's the best person to stay. She'd be the best one to judge how deeply Mrs. Green was falling for Jackman's pitch."

"Ask him," said Karen, "how he thinks I'd be able to communicate my findings to him and Wacko, when *you're* off on a junket in London. Ask him right *now!*"

And again, in less than two minutes this time, she was wishing she'd kept quiet.

"By using the Ear Code, of course," said Buzz.

Karen might have kicked him, if she hadn't been a ghost. Buzz had said it so smugly, it seemed. After all, the Ear Code had been his idea. It was based on the fact that no matter how hard a ghost hit a living person, that person would feel nothing but a very faint cool brush—like the touch of a fly. Which is what most living persons thought it had been, if they ever became conscious of such a contact at all.

"But if that person *knows* about this," Buzz had said,

30

back on Day One of his becoming a squad member, "and if the ghost's touch is directed at a certain spot on the body—prearranged by them both—well then, they can communicate without the word processor. Very crudely, I admit. But good in an emergency."

So they had evolved the code, where the living person asks the ghost a yes/no question, and the ghost replies with a touch on the right ear for yes and on the left for no.

"But this could get too complicated for yes/no questions," said Karen, appealing to Joe. "We're talking about a woman's *heart* here. Her feelings. Her—her—what are you grinning at?"

"It's all right, Karen. I believe you. And anyway"—he turned to Danny and Carlos—"we can *all* go. All the ghosts, that is. Because I've been thinking, and the only developments here that could cause an emergency would be if Mrs. Green decided to marry Jackman. Right?"

Karen nodded.

"I guess so," murmured Danny.

"Sure, sure!" said Carlos, brightening.

"Now Buzz knows Danny's family," Joe went on. "Especially the two older kids. Surely he'll be able to find out from them if anything like that was decided. And Wacko will help him to keep an eye on Jackman himself. Meanwhile, it shouldn't take us long to get some hard information over in London. Seeing that we know his Hampstead address and all."

"Great! Yeah, yeah! I'll tell them now!" said Carlos, turning to the keyboard. But then he swung back to Joe, his face dejected again. "Uh-oh! How will Buzz and Wacko let *us* know, when we're in London? If there *is* an emergency, I mean?"

Joe's grin broadened.

"I've been thinking of that, too. Put those two on hold, and I'll explain."

When Joe had done that, and his idea had been transmitted to Buzz and Wacko, there were big smiles on all six faces.

"So that settles it," said Buzz. "You four go to London, and we'll keep an eye on things at this end."

"Yeah," said Wacko. "I kind of envy you guys, for once. I mean, being ghosts, you won't have to pay a cent for your trip!"

"He's right!" said Carlos. "And we can take our pick of all the flights to London. All the flights on all the airlines."

"We can travel *first class!*" said Karen.

"We'll do better than that," said Joe. "We'll travel first class plus the fastest. How about New York to London in just over three and a half hours?"

"Hey! Wow! Yes!" Carlos was jumping up and down already. "You—you're talking about—"

"Yeah!" said Joe. "I'm talking about *Concorde!*"

6
"What's *Happening* to Us?"

Early the following morning, the four ghosts left town in the back seats of the day's first airport limousine. There were only three living passengers, so there was plenty of room inside.

It wouldn't have mattered if there hadn't been. Because in that case, the four would simply have ridden on the outside, probably on the roof. No matter how fast the limo went, or how bumpy the road, they wouldn't have fallen off. The rush of air makes no difference to a ghost. Even a gale would be unable to blow a single hair out of place—unless the ghost *chose* to let it do that, so he'd feel more at home among living people.

In the same way, they could have sat right up front on the roof, with their legs dangling over the windshield. Being invisible to the driver, their limbs wouldn't have impeded his view one little bit. But there again, a ghost usually prefers not to do such a thing. He knows that the sight of his legs even apparently blocking the view would make himself and any other ghosts around feel very uncomfortable.

"Do things as naturally as possible" was Joe's first advice to any new ghost. "That way, you'll waste much less of the energy or whatever it is that keeps us going efficiently."

That morning, as they sat in the limo, Joe was in no mood for giving out any serious lessons in ghostcraft. Despite the urgency of their mission, they were all in a state of bubbling excitement. Even Danny. After all, this was going to be a first for them in many ways. As ghosts, none of them had ever traveled by air before. Even as living people, only two of them— Joe and Karen—had ever been up in planes. Sure, Joe had actually been on a transatlantic flight once—to Rome, on his honeymoon.

"But it was only in a 747," he said.

"Only!" said Karen, whose flights had been limited to two—from Bradley Field to Boston and back—in much smaller aircraft.

"But now we're all going supersonic!" said Carlos. "Twice the speed of sound! Oh, boy! Oh, boy!"

"Did you say *twice?*" Danny asked.

"That's right!" said Carlos. "Mach 2!"

"Mark *Who?*"

"Mach—that's m-a-c-h. Mach 1 is the speed of sound. That's 760 miles an hour in air just above sea level. Faster than that, way up at the altitude we'll be flying. And at Mach 2, we'll be doing over 1500 miles an hour. Faster than a rifle bullet."

Even to ghosts, Carlos's facts and figures seemed awesome.

They spent the rest of the journey to the airport in silence.

None of them had expected anyone else from their town to be traveling on Concorde. Not at the fare that Wacko had quoted after he'd called the travel agent to check on the flight departure times. But one of the limo passengers had booked a seat on the British Airways regular subsonic flight that left around the same time (and reached London four hours later than Concorde). So the ghosts had no trouble getting to the British Airways terminal. The limousine dropped them at the door.

And, of course, when they got inside, they had no bags to check in, no tickets to show, no passports to bother with.

They simply followed the signs from the Concorde check-in desk and went straight to the Concorde lounge, bypassing the security X-ray check.

"I wonder if *we'd* have shown up on that thing?" said Carlos. "I mean, in any way at all?"

But right then, they were all too excited to take much interest in Carlos's scientific speculations. And once inside the lounge, their excitement took on a different dimension.

It was very quiet in there and very luxurious. Most of the passengers who'd arrived earlier were already settling down to sip the free drinks and nibble the delicious-looking snacks set out for them. But this wasn't what caused the extra excitement.

"Hey! See who *that* is, over there?"

"Isn't he—?"

"Oh, and that lady with the dark glasses! Surely she's—"

Like any living people of their ages and backgrounds, the ghosts found themselves celebrity-watching.

Many of the passengers were businessmen, smartly dressed, already discussing deals in low voices or looking over papers crammed with facts and figures. But it was the casually dressed, even shabby ones who attracted the most attention from the ghosts.

As Joe pointed out:

"People who can pay this kind of money and still not care how sloppily they're dressed, they just have to be celebrities."

So they played their hunches, claiming that this one was a movie star or that one a world-champion golfer or another a singing superstar or another a two-million-dollar-a-year model—each ghost's guess being influenced by what had turned him or her on in life. And maybe they were right or maybe they were wrong. It was hard to be sure, except in one case.

"I *told* you!" said Danny, clapping his hands, after an attendant had come up and addressed a quiet elderly man by name, telling him he was wanted on the phone. "That *is* the guy who starred in all those horror movies!"

As they watched the world-famous actor go to the bank of telephones—that mild pleasant man who'd

36

played so many vampires, monsters, reawakened mummies, mad scientists, evil geniuses and loathsome aliens from distant galaxies—Joe chuckled.

"If only he knew who was traveling with him today, *he'd* be the one with goose bumps!"

But just then, Carlos found a window that gave a good view of the awaiting aircraft: vast, silvery, beautiful, sparkling in the sun, with its nose cone dipped like the beak of some fabulous bird. And their excitement took yet another turn.

"That's it, fellas, there she is! I mean, just look at those lines. I mean, hey! Wow!"

"We—we're going on *that?*" said Danny, awestricken all over again.

"You bet!" said Joe.

"I wish that stuck-up Carol-Jean Van Buren next door could see me now!" sighed Karen.

Then Joe brought them back to reality.

"Listen," he said. "They'll be boarding soon. And when they start, *we* hang back. OK?"

"But why?" said Carlos, jigging with eagerness to get closer acquainted with the aircraft. "*We* don't have to sneak around like regular stowaways. No one can see *us*. We—"

"Because," said Joe, firmly and calmly, "if we go in last, we'll see where the vacant seats are. Then we won't be taking seats that these people have already booked. And so we won't have to keep getting up to make room for them."

None of the others laughed and asked what difference it made. They knew only too well that when a living person sits on a ghost it can be a very unpleasant experience. Not for the living person, who'd feel nothing except a slight coolness—a coolness that might cause a shiver, but only if that person were extrasensitive.

No. It was the ghost who found it unpleasant: a warm, throbbing, suffocating feeling that could linger for hours.

"You're right, Joe," said Carlos, simmering down.

By the time the plane was ready for takeoff, the four had settled in their seats, well back in the rear section. They had managed to find a whole row unoccupied—two seats on each side of the aisle. They'd been rather lucky in this, since the flight was fairly well booked, with single passengers being spaced out so that each one would, in effect, occupy two seats. But although all the seats cost the same fare, and the service was the same throughout, the passengers had tended to avoid the very far end of the plane, probably associating it with the cheapest seats on regular aircraft.

The ghosts didn't mind a bit, just so long as they were all together. In fact, there was even a bonus, in that Danny and Joe had the great horror star directly in front of them, while the person in front of Carlos and Karen was the woman in dark glasses.

"And she *is* who I thought she was!" said Karen, craning to look over the woman's shoulder at the glossy magazine she was slowly leafing through. "One of the world's top models."

"Could have fooled me," said Joe, glancing across at the rather dowdy, terribly skinny young woman.

"I can tell by the way she murmurs or groans every time she turns to one of her own pictures," said Karen.

"Be quiet," said Carlos, "we're starting to move."

Then came the preliminaries: the slow taxiing to the runway; the captain's welcoming chat over the intercom, giving details of the route, the altitude and the expected time of arrival; followed by the attendant's demonstration of the lifesaving apparatus.

Naturally, the last wasn't of much interest to the four passengers who no longer had lives to be saved. But the small dark screen on the wall at the side of the attendant *was* interesting.

It was already flickering with electronic digits: 0.21, 0.22, 0.23 . . .

"That's the Mach speed indicator," said Carlos. "When it gets up to 1.00, we'll be flying at the speed of sound."

"But that won't be until we're away from the coastline," said Joe, continuing to watch the indicator nevertheless.

Danny was sitting next to the window. The aircraft, now fully airborne, was banking somewhat, giving him a view of the ground, with its rows of houses and roads looking like a lot of matchboxes set among ribbons. That was sight enough for him.

"Oh boy!" he murmured softly.

And he was still continuing to gaze out of the window, quite a while later, fascinated this time by glimpses of sunlit clouds far below him, when Joe nudged him and he heard Carlos say:

"That's it! That's it! We've just gone through the sound barrier. Mach 1."

"Carlos!" said Karen, reproachfully. "We can read!"

Danny began to stare at the indicator, which was already flicking to 1.15.

Still Carlos couldn't contain himself. Bobbing up and down in his seat, he kept up his running commentary.

"Look at the rate the numbers are going up now—steadily—fast and steadily—wow!"

They were all staring at the little screen by then, watching the numbers climb and marveling at the smoothness and quietness inside the aircraft. They might have believed it to be stationary, on level ground, if it hadn't been for those steadily changing, flickering numbers.

And it wasn't until the indicator was reading 2.05, and Carlos had yelled that they were now doing *twice* the speed of sound, for Pete's sake, and was asking how about that, huh?—it wasn't until then that Karen finally took her eyes off the screen.

She'd been meaning to crane forward again and see how the woman in front was getting on with her magazine.

But she never made it.

She took one glance at Carlos and screamed.

It was a scream that would have had every flight attendant on board running to see what had happened, if Karen hadn't been a ghost.

Then:

"Look!" she gasped, staring in horror at the others. "Oh, my God! What's *happening* to us?"

7

Mr. Jackman
Plans a Picnic

At that very moment, when Karen had gasped out her question and the airspeed indicator was leveling out at 2.10, the digital clock on the wall of the bank opposite the railroad station back home flicked to 10:30 A.M., and Buzz Phillips asked roughly the same question—though in a much calmer tone:

"I wonder what they're doing right now?"

"Huh! Watching the in-flight movie, I imagine," Wacko Williams replied, without taking his eyes off the street corner, a few yards away from the bank.

The two boys were perched on the guardrail at the edge of the station parking lot. They'd been there for nearly an hour, and Wacko was beginning to feel that there were better ways of spending one's time on a warm summer morning.

"Movie?" said Buzz. "They don't show movies on

Concorde. There just wouldn't be time to do that *and* serve a fancy meal."

Wacko grinned.

"They'll probably be feeling pretty sore, then. Remember what Carlos once told us? About how ghosts don't need to eat and drink—and couldn't even if they tried—but that old habits die hard, and they still sometimes get hunger pangs at the sight of really tempting food."

"Yeah. Anyway, let's hope they managed to get on the thing. Let's hope they had no problems with closed doors and stuff like that."

"Oh, they'll be on it!" said Wacko. "Carlos isn't the sort of guy to—uh-oh! Looks like we've got some action at last."

Two kids had just turned the corner of the street, pushing a battered shopping cart. The cart was empty, but the kids both had a grip on the handle—as if they were setting out on an important errand, and they both wanted to play the leading part.

"Those are the two youngest Green kids, aren't they?" asked Wacko.

Buzz shook his head.

"No. That's Mike and Jilly. The eldest—believe it or not. Very undersized. Mike's ten, and Jilly's eight. . . . I wonder what they're looking so uptight about?"

The two kids were pushing the cart along Railroad Street now. The steering was very erratic, partly due to the tug-of-war going on between them. If the wheels hadn't been so squeaky and acted as a warning signal, some of the pedestrians in front might not have side-stepped in time.

"OK," said Buzz. "Let's have a chat with them. Only remember what Danny said. Don't start grilling them direct. They clam up if you do. Just steer the conversation gently along the way we want it to go."

"I'll leave it to you," said Wacko, following Buzz.

"Hi, Mike! Hi, Jilly!"

The squeaking stopped as the kids pulled up and looked behind them. Their pale, thin faces looked cleaner than Buzz had ever seen them before. Their clothes looked cleaner, too. Brand-new, in fact.

"Hey! I like your T-shirts!" he said.

Jilly's face brightened a little.

"Mine's got red stripes," she said.

"He can see *that*, dummy!" said Mike. "Hi, Buzz! Who's he?"

"I am *not* a dummy!" said Jilly, scowling at her brother.

"Of course you're not, honey," said Buzz. "This is Wacko, Mike. He's—he was a friend of Danny's too."

At the mention of Danny, Jilly's face softened, and her eyes began to fill up. Mike began to smile.

"Hi!" he said to Wacko. He frowned slightly. "How come I never saw you with Danny?"

"He doesn't live around here," said Buzz. "He was Danny's friend at school."

Mike's frown quivered.

"Oh—yeah—sure." Then the frown deepened again. "*You* don't live around here, either. But you used to be with Danny down here all the time."

"Yes, well—Danny and I were *special* friends. . . . Anyway, you look like you're going someplace special with that cart, so we'll—"

Both kids were nodding.

"Picnic!" said Jilly.

"Deli!" said Mike.

Buzz grinned.

"Picnic? Deli? Can't you make up your minds?"

"*Both!*" said Mike, firmly. "We're going to the deli to get the stuff for the picnic."

"Picnic, huh?" said Wacko. "That sounds real nice."

"Yeah," said Jilly. "Mr. Whosis is taking us all—me, Mom, him, Arnie and Sylvia."

"Don't call him that!" said Mike. "It's Mr. Jackman. Jack-man. OK? Say it!"

"Jaxman," said Jilly, still looking up at Buzz and Wacko. "And he's taking us in a big station wagon he's rented. He's coming for us at eleven-thirty."

"Hey, yeah!" said Mike, starting to push. "We'd better get going. So long, Buzz. So long—"

"That's OK," said Buzz. Ever since the name Jackman had been mentioned, he and Wacko had been extra-alert. "We're going that way, too."

"I guess you'll be taking your swimsuits along, day like this," said Wacko. "Down by the lake, it should be just—"

"Aren't going to the lake," said Mike.

"We don't have any swimsuits," said Jilly. "We can't swim anyway so—"

"*You* can't, and Arnie and Sylvia can't," said Mike, indignantly. "I *can!*"

"You can only swim if someone holds you—"

"We're going on a treasure hunt!" said Mike, loudly, partly in triumph, partly to get his sister to change the subject.

44

The two older boys glanced at each other. Both were thinking the same thing—remembering Carlos's and Danny's account of the telephone conversation and the box of old papers.

"Hey! Wow! Whose idea was that?" said Buzz.

"His," said Jilly.

"Whose? Mike's?"

"No! Mr. Whos— Mr. Jaxman's."

"Yeah," said Mike. "We're having a picnic up in the hills. Sentinel Pass. There's a pond there and just a couple of tables, and *she* cried because she'd rather go to the picnic place by the big lake and play in the sand."

"I did *not* cry!"

"But Mr. Jackman said there was something very special up there, some buried treasure, so he's going to give us all some big sticks to poke around with."

"A treasure hunt," said Jilly.

"I guess what he's done," said Mike confidentially to Buzz and Wacko, "is he's already gone up there this morning to hide the stuff for us to find."

"Sounds like a nice guy," said Wacko.

Mike nodded, but said nothing.

"*Is* he, Jilly?" said Wacko.

The little girl shrugged.

"I guess," she murmured.

Buzz studied their faces.

Either the Green kids had clammed up under too much pressure, as Danny had warned—or there was something about Jackman they weren't sure of, despite his picnics and his treats.

They'd reached the deli by now.

"Sentinel Pass," said Buzz, pretending to be thoughtful. "Why, isn't that where we were going to take a bike ride this afternoon, Wacko?"

"Were we?" said Wacko. Then he smiled. "Oh, sure—yes!"

"Oh, well, we might be seeing you around then," said Mike. "Come on, Jilly, or we'll never make it for when Mr. Jackman comes to pick us up."

As the two Ghost Squad members walked away, Wacko said:

"We could be wasting our time, of course. I mean *we're* not like the others. We'll never be able to get close enough to the guy to find out what he's planning."

"I know," said Buzz. "I still can't help wishing at least one of them had stayed behind. For the real close work." Then, after they'd walked on in silence for a couple of minutes, he stared up into the clear blue sky and frowned. "I wonder how the other four *are* doing, though? I mean right now. I can't help having a kind of uneasy feeling—"

"Baloney!" said Wacko, laughing. "You worry too much!"

"Yeah!" sighed Buzz. Then he laughed, too. "I guess I must have caught it from Danny. . . . Anyway, about this afternoon . . ."

His uneasy feeling faded as they started to make their plans.

8
The Corrugation Factor

The sight that met Danny's eyes when he turned from the airspeed indicator to see what had caused Karen's scream nearly set him screaming, too.

"What—?" he gasped, before his voice became choked with horror.

For Karen's face was indeed a picture. Not an oil painting, either.

It was like a very distorted TV picture, with horizontal lines across it—deep grooves and ridges. And not only her face. Her hair and arms and shirt— everything about her seemed to have undergone the same change.

Then— "Oh, *no!*" Danny groaned, turning to look at Joe and Carlos, after being aroused by similar groans from them.

They too had been afflicted in the same way!

Danny forced himself to look down at his hands and immediately felt on the brink of passing out.

He hadn't escaped, either!

Close up, the ridges and grooves looked rather like the kind that a corduroy cushion makes on living flesh when someone presses a cheek against it. Except in this case it would have taken a very tough corduroy, with unusually thick cords, to have bitten that deep.

"It—it's just *us*," muttered Joe. "Everybody else is OK. Look!"

The horror star in front of them still looked the same. So did the model across the aisle. So did all the other passengers in that section, as they happily sipped their drinks or listened to music through their earphones or read their magazines or business papers. So did the flight attendants as they moved about, smiling, anticipating the passengers' needs.

Danny felt especially annoyed at the actor's immunity. Even in his terror, he found himself thinking that there they were—himself and his three partners—looking far more horrible than the actor had ever been made to look.

"Even when he was the mad scientist and his flesh began to turn to fungus! And now he's sitting there, good as new!"

"It's just us ghosts!" said Carlos, repeating what Joe had said, but in a slightly less horrified tone.

Only Karen was feeling as bad as she had at the first shock.

"I'll be disfigured for *life!*" she wailed, gingerly feeling her face with the tips of her fingers.

Nobody commented on how funny those words

sounded, coming from a ghost. Nobody was feeling in the mood for laughs.

But gradually a steadier, calmer reaction was beginning to set in. Grim, yes—but more courageous, even curious.

Joe set the tone, by turning to Carlos.

"What do you think's happened? Something—uh—scientific? Maybe just a passing effect?"

Carlos was studying his own body.

"Could be, yeah," he muttered. "It's affected our clothes, see, not just our skins. And yet it isn't a visual effect—something affecting only our eyes and causing us to see things this way. Otherwise all these other folks would be—uh—corrugated, too."

"*Corrugated?* Oh, my—"

"Take it easy, Karen," said Joe. "Let's hear what Carlos thinks."

"Sure!" Karen shut her eyes and took a deep breath. "Sorry, Carlos. Go ahead."

"Well, it could be a side effect of supersonic speed. Or altitude. I don't know. Some sort of—uh—Corrugation Factor." Karen shuddered. Carlos continued: "I wish I'd had advance warning, then I could have pinpointed just when it started—which Mach number."

"I wish *I'd* had advance warning!" said Karen, still with her eyes stubbornly shut. "I'd have stayed behind with Buzz and Wacko!"

"Anyway," said Carlos, "I don't know about you guys, but except for the way we *look*, I feel fine. My educated guess is that as soon as we go subsonic it'll pass."

"Educated *hope*, you mean, don't you?"

Joe frowned at Carlos and shook his head, warning him to ignore Karen's remarks. She still had her eyes shut, but she had stopped feeling her face. Two of her fingers, ridged like fancy-cut french fries, were tightly crossed.

"How about *you* guys?" said Carlos. "Do *you* feel OK, except for the shock?"

"Well—uh—" Danny looked around again, taking care to keep his eyes off his own body and the appearance of the other three. "Well—sure—I mean—"

"We'll run a few tests," said Carlos, springing up and standing in the aisle.

And so he led the way, checking out how they felt standing, walking, moving their arms. He even hustled Karen into doing these things.

"Good!" he murmured. "Locomotor systems seem unaffected, anyway. Now let's make sure there's no visual impairment. Starting with color . . ."

The tests continued, including hearing, touching (though only of each other) and smelling. The smelling test was rather inconclusive in some cases, because, like taste, the sense of smell is very weak in ghosts at the best of times. In fact, some ghosts believe it's an illusory sense—that a ghost only *thinks* he can smell certain things, out of old habit, reinforced by memories.

"This seems to support that theory," said Carlos, after Karen had taken deep sniffs at the horror star's glass of whiskey and declared she could smell nothing. "Karen's one of those who normally thinks she can smell things, right?"

"Sure—but . . ." She sniffed again. "Not now."

Carlos smiled.

"That's because you've just had a big shock," he said. "It's upset all your normal memory links. Just swamped them for the time being. But you'll be OK. Don't worry."

Carlos was really enjoying himself by now. Once his scientific curiosity was aroused, it wouldn't have mattered even if he'd sprouted an extra head. He'd have been just as eager to find out the cause.

Danny was also feeling easier. Carlos's cool, systematic checking had done a lot to calm his nerves. It seemed to have had the same effect on the others, too. Including Karen.

"Well, I'm glad *you* didn't stay back home, anyway, Carlos," she said eventually, and she even managed a small brave smile.

But the grooves and ridges didn't go away, and it was still very worrying. They spent the next ninety minutes or so in near silence, only speaking and moving whenever Carlos thought of some other small, more refined test to subject them to.

Then the Mach numbers on the screen began to drop.

"This is it!" said Carlos, crouching forward, causing Danny to feel as if his heart had skipped a beat and Karen to shut her eyes tight again.

Danny kept his open, however.

Holding his furrowed hand in front of his face so that he could see both it and the indicator at the same time, he watched anxiously.

1.95 . . . 1.90 . . . 1.87 . . .

The numbers were continuing to go down.

But the ridges weren't. The grooves were still as deep as ever.

Or—were they?

1.70 . . . 1.69 . . . 1.68 . . . 1.67 . . .

He switched the focus of his eyes to his hand.

Was it his imagination—his desperately hopeful imagination—or were the grooves beginning to look less distinct?

At his side, he heard Joe catch his breath.

Across the aisle, Carlos began to say something in tones that were low and cautious for him, more like a muttered prayer really. But the words were drowned by the captain's voice, over the loudspeakers.

"We are now reducing speed as we approach the coast of Wales. In just over thirty minutes, we shall be landing at Heathrow Airport, touching down at approximately 6:00 P.M. British Summer Time. This is ten minutes ahead of schedule and exactly three hours and thirty minutes after leaving JFK. . . . If you haven't adjusted your watches already, please remember to put them forward by five hours. . . ."

The indicator was still continuing to drop.

Danny was almost certain now that the grooves were beginning to smooth out.

"The weather in London is fine," the captain continued, "with only a slight overcast. The temperature is seventy-eight degrees Fahrenheit. We hope you've enjoyed your flight on supersonic Concorde and that you will travel with us again. The flight attendants shall now proceed to . . ."

The four ghosts were too intent on observing one

another to pay any further attention to the captain. The speed had just fallen below Mach 1, and was still dropping.

"Yes, I think—yeah! It *is!* It's beginning to wear off already!" said Carlos.

"Are you sure?" asked Karen, her eyes lighting up.

"Positive! Forget it! It's nothing. I told you. It's just like getting creases from a pillow."

"Thank goodness for that!" said Karen, beginning to smile.

"Amen!" murmured Joe.

"Yeah!" grunted Danny.

The ridges were still with them, but much less noticeable, when they landed. As they threaded their way through the other passengers in the immigration and passport-control area, they began to turn their attention to practical details.

"Our next problem," said Joe, "is how to get from here to Hampstead."

"We could walk it," said Karen. "Why not? The way I'm feeling right now I could *dance* it!"

She smiled down at the fading furrows on her brown arms.

"What?" said Carlos. "Ten, twelve miles—maybe more? Forget it!"

"There's got to be public transportation," said Danny.

"Sure!" said Carlos. "I mean, being ghosts, the walk wouldn't tire us any. But think of the time. We want to get there while it's still daylight."

By now they were going through the baggage claim

area, where passengers from earlier flights were still crowding around the slowly moving conveyor belts laden with bags and suitcases.

"One thing," said Joe, "we don't have to hang around waiting for bags."

"Or open up for customs," said Carlos as they headed for the exits, where customs officials were busy. "Look at that poor guy over—oops! Sorry!"

He'd just bumped into a young woman. She was dressed in an airline uniform, but not the same kind as the girls on their own plane.

"That's all right," said the woman, smiling.

She had very dark hair and eyes. The smile was warm, but the eyes had a curious look as they glanced at the four ghosts.

"Hey!" said Carlos. "Seeing that you felt it when I bumped into you, it means that *you're*—"

"A ghost also?" said the woman, with a faint sad sigh. "Yes. . . ." Then she brightened up. "And *you've* all just flown in on Concorde, right?"

"Yes," said Joe. He glanced around. Most of the passengers in that area had obviously come in on different flights, from widely different places. "How did you guess?"

"The creases," said the woman. "It always happens when a ghost flies supersonic."

"Does it—?" Karen began, looking anxious again.

"Wear off completely? Sure! It will be gone inside another hour."

"You've seen this before, then?" said Joe.

"Quite a few times, yes. Mind you, there still aren't many ghosts who've—how do you say?—latched onto

54

traveling by air *commercially*. But there are those who are interested in military aircraft. And when they steal rides on supersonic bombers, they come out with the creases, just like you."

"Hey!" said Carlos. "You don't mean there are ghost *spies*, do you?"

The woman smiled.

"Yes," she said. "They just can't resist it. Of course, it's not a scrap of use to them or their governments. Because"—she sighed—"as you must know very well, there is simply no way of passing the information on to the living."

"Er—no," said Joe, giving Carlos a quick frown, when he looked about to say something. "Anyway," he continued, *"we're* not government agents."

"No," said the woman, smiling warmly again. "I can see that. You're just sight-seeing, I suppose? Well, it's as good a way as any to pass the time."

"How about you—uh—Miss—?"

"Irma," said the woman. "Irma Shavit. And your names?"

After he'd answered this question, Joe continued with his own.

"Are you just passing the time, too?"

Irma's face clouded. All the brightness drained from her eyes and mouth.

"No. I—I stay around here because—well—"

Then, in a few words, she told them the story of her afterlife: how she'd been a flight attendant on her country's national airline; how it was a major target for terrorists; how she'd been killed, not far from that very spot, when she and other members of the same crew had been boarding the limousine that was to have taken them to their hotel.

"Terrorists?"

"Yes. Hand grenades and machine-gun fire. We didn't have a chance." She sighed. "I'm afraid London has become the European center for terrorism. And"—her eyes hardened—"that's why I stay around here. Like the spies, I suppose. The ones we were laughing at just now. I listen to the conversations of people I know to be mixed up in terrorist activities. I just can't keep myself from trying to find out what they're plotting next."

"I know how you must feel," said Joe.

"Do you? Really? Then you must know how frustrated I get—knowing that if I ever did uncover a similar plot—well—what would *I* be able to do about it?"

"There *are* ways, you know," said Carlos, before Joe could check him. "I mean, like—"

"Like telepathy?" said Irma. She sighed. "Yes. Well, that's what I'm counting on. You see, my younger sister also works as a flight attendant, and I'm dreading the day that I should ever find out about a plot to attack *her* flight. In fact, there is something being cooked up even now that might—" She broke off and shrugged. "But—well—I just will have to cross that bridge when I get to it."

"Big bridge!" murmured Karen.

"The biggest!" said Irma. "Anyway"—she forced a smile—"I am keeping you from your sights. Were you heading for any place in particular? Do you know London? Can I help you at all?"

Irma was now all flight attendant again, anxious to be of assistance—and no doubt using her old life-habits and routines to take her mind off her present anxieties and despairs.

"Hampstead?" she said. "Why, yes. I often stayed in that area. What you require is the Underground. Without a doubt, it is the easiest and quickest for ghosts as well as the living. So long as you remember where to change. Come with me, and I'll show you the best routes."

So saying, she led them to a big map of the London Underground system on a nearby wall. A large clock just above it registered 6:25.

"That's—uh—*one* twenty-five back home," Danny told himself. "I wonder if Buzz and Wacko have made any progress yet?"

9
The Blighted Bowl

The long, twisting uphill road to Sentinel Pass was hardly the ideal route for a bicycle ride. Besides being very steep for much of the way, its surface was so pitted and scarred that it might as well have been a dirt road.

"In fact a dirt road would at least have been fairly *even!*" grumbled Wacko, losing his balance as his front wheel hit another pothole.

"You should look where you're going," grunted Buzz, continuing his tacking from side to side.

Then he struck a pothole himself and went sprawling into the bank.

Wacko was too bushed to do more than grin.

Wiping the sweat off his forehead and beating at a small cloud of gnats, he said:

"Anyway, we should be nearly there by now. Surely this next bend'll be the last!"

The bugs were bothering Buzz, too.

"The trouble with trees," he said, "is they shade you from the sun, but they swarm with bugs. They—"

He stopped, leaned on his handlebars, and said:

"Listen! Did you hear that?"

"What?"

"Sounded like a man's voice—yes! There!"

From somewhere up above them, around the bend and through the trees, a hoarse but loud voice was barking orders.

"Not *there*, you little fool! Over *here!*"

Wacko shrugged.

"Sounds mad."

"What do you bet it isn't the smooth and sweet-talking Mr. Jackman?" said Buzz.

When they'd rounded the bend, they were relieved to find that they were at last within sight of their destination. The road leveled out, and the trees became less dense—crowded out by numerous gray boulders that were scattered around on the land at either side.

"Well, there's the pond and the picnic area," said Buzz, stopping again and nodding to the spot some three or four hundred yards along the road.

The water gleamed in the sun there, through the trunks of a ragged line of pines, where the boys could also make out the glitter of a parked car and glimpses of dull red picnic tables.

"But where are they all?"

Wacko stared around, feeling somewhat repelled. There was something about that spot that seemed forbidding, even on a bright afternoon. Maybe it was the looming twin peaks of Sentinel Mountain, dark

59

with evergreens—between which the road continued to wind, uphill again, to the Pass itself.

Wacko tried to remember what he'd heard about it. Something about a British Army encampment during the Revolution—on another plateau, now wooded over, beyond the Pass. And a village of some kind on this side. And a battle here, in which the pond had turned crimson, and had even crusted over, with blood. Port Wine Pond, some of the old folks still called it. And tales of angry ghosts, thirsting for revenge—because it had not been a clean battle, but one shot through and through with treachery of one kind or another . . .

"There—he's yelling again," said Buzz. "But where? Do you see anyone?"

They listened.

"How many more times, idiot? Over here!"

The voice was more distinct now—close enough for them to catch its tones. It was the voice of a man with very nasty temper.

"Ah!" said Buzz, as they slowly advanced. "Well, there's Mrs. Green, anyway."

From the point they'd now reached, the woman could be seen sitting at one of the two picnic tables. The table itself was piled with cartons, cans and Styrofoam containers. The woman was just pouring herself another drink from a tall, dark green bottle.

"She's happy enough," said Wacko. "But where's—"

"Mr. Jaxman! Is this it?"

"That was Jilly's voice," said Buzz. "And it seemed to come from over there."

He pointed to a slight rise in the field at their side.

60

"Oh, don't be such a little fool!" came the rasp of a man's voice.

"Yes," said Wacko. "Let's take a peek."

Leaving their bikes at the side of the road, the boys climbed the gentle slope, picking their way through the boulders and between the trees. Then:

"Well, what d'you know!" drawled Buzz. "The Jackman Treasure Hunt in full swing!"

The land at the other side of the rise fell away more sharply, into a wide, shallow, natural bowl. And here the scene was even more forbidding than back under the shadow of Sentinel Pass. There had once been living trees here, too, covering the whole area of the bowl, but all that was left were rows of blackened dead stumps and dry leafless limbs, jagged and ugly as rotten teeth. Even the undergrowth below these vegetable corpses was stunted and gray-looking—though obviously still tough and wiry.

"It's scratchy!" wailed a kid's voice.

"Shut up and keep going!" snarled the man's.

"So *that's* Jackman!" murmured Buzz.

The treasure seekers had their backs toward the observers. Each of them had a long thick cane—in the case of the two youngest kids, the canes were longer than they were—and they were slowly moving forward, in line abreast, with a space of three or four feet between them. The kids were stumbling and straggling, the man was stomping, and all of them were prodding, prodding, prodding—probing the undergrowth with the canes.

"He *looks* like a jerk!" said Buzz.

Wacko grunted. He could see what his partner

meant. There was something very repulsive about the well-pressed neatness of the man's jeans and the way his expensive rugby shirt—too clinging for such a pudgy figure—betrayed the rolls of flab.

"I wonder what they're *really* looking for?" he murmured.

"I don't know, but whatever it is, the kids seem to have lost interest."

"Who wouldn't, with him yapping at them like that?" said Wacko.

"Anyway, I only count three kids. Was there another over at the picnic tables?" said Buzz.

"None that I could see. And—hey—it looks like Mike is the missing one. I don't see *him*."

"No. I wonder— Look out! I think they're turning this way. Let's edge around to the side."

As the boys retreated, out of sight of Jackman and the kids, and began to make their way around the rim of the blighted bowl, they heard another sound, closer to them.

"Do you hear what I hear?" Buzz whispered, grabbing Wacko's arm. "Just over there? Behind that bush?"

Wacko nodded.

"Yeah. Someone crying. I think we've found Mike. Come on."

Sure enough, there sat Mike, on a boulder, sniffling and blinking up at them through his tears.

"Hi, Mike!"

"Huh—oh—hi . . ."

Mike didn't seem surprised. He looked too upset even to notice anything unusual in their coming across him like that, so far from the road.

"What's the trouble, Mike?"

Mike looked up at Buzz and glared through his tears. "Root cellars!" he said.

It was so unexpected that both boys glanced at each other uneasily.

"What's that again?" said Buzz.

"Root cellars! Stinking lousy root cellars!" said Mike, indignantly. "*That's* not buried treasure!"

"You mean that's what he's got you all prodding for?"

"Yeah. He says there used to be some old houses down there. With stone cellars. And we had to push and poke around and get scratched and bit and poison-ivyed, just for that."

"Sounds pretty dull, I guess," Buzz said sympathetically, though casting a quick glance at Wacko again, to see if the other was thinking what he was thinking.

"The treasure," murmured Wacko. "Yeah."

"Treasure!" growled Mike. "Some treasure! Some roots in some old cellar! Even if there *is* a cellar there. And dull—yeah!" He glared at Buzz again. "And hard, and boring, and—and . . ."

His voice trailed off. He was staring at something behind them. Suddenly his anger had drained away. Now he just looked scared.

They turned.

Jackman himself was approaching. City-dweller though he looked in his phony country clothes, he certainly had the knack of moving silently. Like a seasoned hunter.

"So *there* you are!" he said, his voice husky and

sugary again, staring down at Mike with a small pursed-up smile that was probably meant to be kindly. But the eyes were cold and snakelike as they slid to take in Buzz and Wacko. "And who are these two gentlemen?"

"They—they're—"

"We were just passing," said Buzz. "And we heard him crying. We thought he might be lost."

"Well, he isn't," said Jackman, reaching down and clamping a soft hand around Mike's wrist. "Come on, Mike." The muscles in that hand must have been pretty hard inside their soft covering, Buzz decided. Judging from the ease with which Mike was pulled to his feet. "Mike, gentlemen, is just a crybaby, that's what Mike is. Just a spoiled Mama's boy—aren't you, Mike?"

"I—I—"

Mike's protest slumped into a sob.

"What you need, my lad, is a bit of discipline. Now stop your sniveling and come join your brother and sisters."

So, without a backward glance at his two sympathizers, Mike was led off.

"Hm! Nice guy!" said Wacko, looking disgusted.

"Yeah." Buzz was looking thoughtful. "I can see now why Danny was so worried."

"Well," said Wacko, "maybe we *should* be rooting for him and his root cellar, at that. Maybe if he does find it, and it *is* full of treasure, maybe he won't need Mrs. Green's money."

Buzz grunted.

"Yeah. Maybe. And maybe not. He looks like just the sort of guy whose greed wouldn't let him rest until he gets *both*."

A deerfly suddenly made a dart at him. He stepped back quickly.

Then he shivered.

"What's wrong?" said Wacko, seeing the startled look on Buzz's face. "The fly get you?"

Buzz shook his head.

"No. It missed. But— No, it's nothing. . . ."

"*What's* nothing?"

"Just one of those cold pockets of air you get sometimes in places like this. Even on a hot day."

Wacko grinned and wiped his forehead.

"So move over, then! I could use some of that cool myself."

But when they'd changed places, the cold air was no more.

"I guess I must have used it up," said Buzz. "Unless—"

"Unless what?"

Buzz grinned sheepishly.

"Unless I just stepped back into one of the others. Remember what Carlos once said about sitting on a ghost? But *they* should be over in London by now. Maybe even in Hampstead."

Wacko glanced at his watch.

"They *could* be," he said. "It's way after seven, British time."

10
The Brother and Sister, Part One: Suspicions

There was nothing desolate about the hill on which the rest of the Ghost Squad found themselves when they emerged from the Underground into the golden evening sunshine. This was a hill seething with activity: crowded with houses, stores, churches, apartment buildings. Every main road was still crawling with traffic, and the sidewalks were flowing with streams of humanity—surging here, eddying there, and occasionally spilling over into the roadway.

"Wow! This is some busy neighborhood!" said Carlos, edging close to the wall of a movie theater.

"Yes—and a fashionable one," said Karen, staring at the women's clothes. "A lot of these are tourists, I guess, but some of them look very well-to-do."

"Not to mention other ghosts," said Joe, as he excused himself to a white-haired gentleman who'd just bumped into him. The elderly ghost grunted and went on his way. "I'd say this was a very popular place with ghosts."

"The more folks who live in a place, the more ghosts there'll be," said Carlos. "It's a statistical certainty, and—"

"And anyway it's an expensive neighborhood, that's for sure," said Danny, impatient to get on with the mission. "So Jackman wasn't kidding about it being a prime location for antique stores. I can see three from where I'm standing now."

Taking the hint, the others moved into action, concentrating on finding the Jackman store, with Danny and Carlos—the only ones who'd seen the picture— in the lead.

None of the three that Danny had spotted was it, but this didn't throw them. The main shopping streets formed a large inverted Y—the two converging branches climbing to the stem branch, which itself continued to climb and twist out of sight—and all these streets had their share of antique stores.

"It was on a corner," said Carlos. "I remember that. So— Hey! There it is! Across the road, a bit farther down."

They all saw it now. The gold lettering over the window gleamed in the sun, as if mocking them for being so slow.

RICHARD JACKMAN
SOLE PROPRIETOR

"It's pretty new," said Joe, peering up at the sign. "There's still a faint trace of an earlier name under it."

"Yeah!" said Carlos. "I think I see a *C* and an *R* under the *J* and *A*."

"And there was an *and* sign, just before the *Sole*," said Karen.

"Looks like a ghost name itself," said Carlos.

"Probably is," said Danny. "The name of a person who is a ghost now." He sighed. "Too bad it's closed."

The storefront was not quite as grand as it had looked in the brochure, but it was one of the largest they'd seen so far. And there was something about the rich, black, glossy paintwork and the heaviness of the glass-paneled door, crisscrossed inside with a gold-colored security grille, that said plainly that this was a very prosperous concern, even before anyone got around to studying the contents of the windows.

"That's OK," Joe said to Danny. "I didn't expect to find it open this late. But there's a lot we can find out just from the outside. The stuff on display sure looks—"

"Do you mind if we move around to the side window?" said Karen. She was glaring at a couple of olive-skinned young men who'd just gone past, laughing and saying something in a foreign language. "I'm tired of being jostled—and by other *ghosts* at that! The tall one just *pinched* me! It's worse than when I was alive!"

She soon calmed down when they'd moved to the second window, around the corner, in the less busy side street.

"That's a nice mirror," she murmured.

It was a very large one, covering almost the top half of the wall facing the window. Its gilt frame was heavy and richly figured with scrolls and cupids and minia-ture urns and wreaths and acorns and oak leaves and rambling roses. But Karen was more interested in her own reflection, as she slowly moved her face from side to side.

"I like that grandfather's clock," said Carlos.

"And if I'm not mistaken, that's a real Persian rug," said Karen, taking some time off from the mirror.

Joe grunted.

"I guess Jackman wasn't lying too much when—"

"Shall we see if any windows are open around the back?" said Danny.

"Save your energy," said Joe. "They don't leave open windows in places like this. If they do, you can be sure they'll be heavily barred on the inside. And that's just as bad for ghost intruders as it is for the living."

"Irma was right," said Karen, back with her reflection. "The furrows have gone completely. Thank goodness ghosts can see their own reflection."

"*I* could have told you about the furrows, if you'd asked," said Carlos, scornfully. "The trouble with you, Karen, is—"

But Carlos never got to deliver his opinion.

"Hold it!"

Something in Joe's voice made them all look at him sharply. He too was staring at the mirror.

"Keep looking in the window," said Joe, still in the same low urgent tones. "All of you. We're being watched."

"Huh?"

Danny suddenly found it tremendously difficult not to swing around.

"Then it must be—?" Carlos began.

"Ghosts. Right."

"Those stupid men again?"

"No, Karen—and don't turn your head!" Joe was still staring at the mirror. "It's two kids. Just across the street. Try to catch their reflection if you can."

Some of the others had to shift their positions slightly. But it didn't take long for them all to see what Joe was talking about.

The boy and the girl across the street were obviously interested in *them*, not the antique store. They were both dark-haired, with large dark eyes and sharply defined, even fierce-looking, eyebrows. The girl was about ten, and the boy, fourteen or fifteen. They were very well dressed, as if for a party—the boy in a neat gray suit with a shirt and tie, the girl in a red velvet dress, a white lace collar and white knee socks. They were obviously brother and sister, and, equally obviously, the boy was having trouble restraining the girl from crossing to get a closer look at them.

"Why don't we just go across ourselves?" said Carlos. "And ask them what's so special about us."

"No!" Joe was very positive. "*One*—there's no need. The fact that we're looking in here, taking such an interest, is special enough, that's for sure. And *Two*—they look so uptight I can almost hear them twanging. One wrong move from us—one sudden move—and they'll run."

"So?" said Karen.

"So right now, since we haven't seemed to notice them, they probably think we're living people. But if they do come across, for Pete's sake *act* like you're living. Don't glance at them. And talk about the stuff in

70

the window, like we're simply killing time. And—"

"They're coming now," said Carlos.

The kids were speaking in low voices. But as they got closer, the four visitors were able to hear what they were saying.

"They seem *too* interested." The girl's voice was clear and firm, even though it was low. And there was a slight but unmistakable viciousness in it. "I mean, they don't look at *all* like regular customers."

"I know, Samantha. That's why it's worth checking on them. But I wish you'd . . ."

The boy's voice was lower and gentler than the girl's. Joe, Karen, Danny and Carlos were jabbering away in loud voices now, talking about the antiques.

Then the girl raised hers.

"Ugh! They're *Americans!* I *hate* Americans!"

The "Americans" found it difficult to maintain their light chatter. One or two of them faltered, but— boosted by Joe's example—managed to keep up the pretense.

"Come *on*, Sam!" the boy was saying. "That's just prejudice."

"I don't care! *He's* American. And I hate—hate— *hate* him!"

Danny felt a prickling sensation at the back of his neck. The only ghosts he'd ever heard speak like that were Malevs—the haters and would-be destroyers, the evil spirits that most people thought of when the subject of ghosts came up. There weren't as many of them as people imagined. But they were very bad news even so—especially to other ghosts.

"Just because Jackman's American," the boy said,

sounding patient but strained, "doesn't mean that all Am—" He broke off. "*Now* what?"

"I don't know, Bern. But when you said Jackman's name, that one with the funny wheel thing on his shirt seemed to listen."

"Don't be silly. How could he? We're ghosts, re-member?"

"Well, anyway, I don't like the look of them." Sa-mantha's voice was firm again, firm and hostile. "What are American *kids* doing looking so interested in an antiques shop anyway? If it had been clothes, it would have made sense, but antiques, no. I think they could be relatives of *his*. So I *still* hate them!"

"He isn't a kid, this big one with the ginger hair who looks like a building worker. He looks too dim to appreciate antiques, I know. But he isn't a kid. And *she* looks quite nice."

The "dim" one was fighting to repress a hot retort, and "she" to keep back a smile, while Samantha's voice dropped a little.

"Well, yes. But"—the girl's voice dropped lower still—"Bernard—this scruffy one. I mean, look at him. Dressed like this, this leather jacket thing. Dressed for cold weather on a day like this. I—"

She screamed. She began to run.

"*They're ghosts! It's a trap!*"

She had touched the sleeve of Danny's wind-breaker—and found that she could feel it.

"Stay where you are!" said Joe to the others. "If we start chasing them now, they'll never have any confi-dence in us. And what they have to tell us could be vital."

Danny gulped.

"You think—?"

"That they're the dead kids Jackman and his buddy were talking about? Yes."

"But we might never get the chance again," said Carlos, staring down the long side street, where the two kids could still be seen: running, dwindling, at the other side of the line of parked cars.

"Don't worry," said Joe. "If my hunch is right, they'll be just as anxious to learn our story as we are to learn theirs. So here's what we do. . . ."

11
The Brother and Sister, Part Two: Their Story

For the next hour or so, the four visitors spent their time wandering around the streets of Hampstead just like any other group of tourists. They moved slowly, seemingly aimlessly, admiring the narrow streets and alleyways and the small, huddled, well-preserved houses, bright with flowers in window boxes and tubs. They strolled along the broader avenues, peering at what looked like medium-sized mansions tucked away behind shrubs and trees. They gazed in the windows of smaller stores they came across in out-of-the-way corners: tiny windows with expensive goods behind them—things to wear or eat or simply to possess and admire.

But as they did all these things, they kept a sharp lookout for signs of Bernard and Samantha, and they weren't disappointed.

The kids never ventured closer than a hundred

yards. Mostly, all that could be seen of them was a pair of dark heads peeking around a corner or above the hood of a parked car. One moment they would be there, but before the one who'd spotted them could alert the others, the kids would be gone, vanished, just the way ghosts were supposed to.

But Danny and the others knew better.

"They're quick, I'll say that for them," said Carlos, as the four stood outside the railings of Keats House, looking down on the long-dead poet's neat old cottage across the garden.

Samantha and Bernard had last shown themselves peeping around the trunk of a gnarled oak tree farther along the road.

"Like forest animals," said Karen, somewhat uneasily.

"Or Indians," said Danny.

"That's because they know the place," said Carlos. "*We* could do that back home, just as good. I mean they belong here. They know all the best hiding places. All they have to do is see which way we're headed, then run on in front and get into the best positions to spy on us."

Joe grinned.

"Yeah! And that suits me fine. Because now that it's getting near sundown, I thought we'd head over to that parklike place we keep seeing at the end of some of these streets. They must be feeling pretty sure of themselves by now—and all the more likely to slip up."

"So?"

"So that's where we'll set our trap. If we just sit around someplace over there, talking quietly, like we mean to stay for hours, they'll be sure to try creeping up on us to hear what we're saying."

The "parklike place" was in fact Hampstead Heath—a huge area of grass and woodland open to the public and stretching for miles, with the city all around it. From some points, on a quiet day, you could imagine you were far away in the country. But from others—the higher, less wooded points—you could see London spread out in a great panorama. And on an evening like this, with the sun going down, drawing sparks from the spires of ancient domes and steeples and blazing dimly on the windows of modern high-rise buildings, it was a breathtaking sight.

Sitting on a grassy slope, with a clump of bushes behind them and the whole of this view at their feet, the four almost forgot that they weren't just regular sightseers.

"Isn't that St. Paul's Cathedral?"

"And there, just to the left, where the sun's shining on some water, that's the Tower of London! Isn't it?"

Karen sighed when, a little later, the reflected sunlight faded away, and the haze over the panorama thickened, and the artificial lights took over, beginning to glitter like strings of jewels along the main thoroughfares down there, or sparkle and twinkle like Christmas tree decorations through the multicolored drapes in the high-rise towers.

"I wish I knew where Buckingham Palace was," she said.

"Why?"

"Because while we're waiting for the Jackman store to open in the morning, we could go over and take a look at the Queen of England in her own home. And maybe Prince Charles and—"

"Hey, *yes!*" Carlos looked excited. "Being ghosts, we can go anywhere. Only the place *I'd* rather go would be the Tower of London and see the crown jewels and maybe some of the resident ghosts they're supposed to have, like the queen that got her head chopped off, and—"

"And that reminds me," said Joe, sternly. "Some of you are getting too steamed up. You'd better cool it or you'll be in trouble! I mean *big* trouble!"

They stared at him.

"Oh, like what, Joe?"

"Like this business of poking your nose into things just out of curiosity. Things that have nothing to do with us or why we're here. Using your ghost advantages for *that* will use up your energy like nothing else can. I've known ghosts who went prying into things that didn't concern them wipe themselves out in a couple of weeks. And going to see what the Queen of England has for her supper or what kind of bath salts she uses—well, it just isn't any concern of ours. Right, Karen?"

"No. Sorry, Joe."

Carlos nudged Danny, grinning at the way Karen was hanging her head.

"That's OK," said Joe. "But that's not the biggest kind of trouble I've had wind of today. *You*, Carlos, have to watch your mouth."

Carlos's grin vanished, but his mouth remained open. "Me?"

"Yeah. *You!* You almost spilled it to Irma back at the airport. About you know what."

"About the way we can—?"

"*There you go again!*" snapped Joe. "Do you realize what would happen if people got to hear of it? Ghosts as well as the living? And when I say ghosts, I'm talking Malevs now. Huh? Can you imagine what would happen? Everyone would want a piece of the action, and Buzz's and Wacko's lives—and our after-lives—wouldn't be worth *that!*"

He snapped his fingers.

It was growing dark, but with their extrastrong night vision the others had no difficulty in making out every grim line and every knotted muscle on Joe's face.

Then it relaxed a little. A twinkle came into his eyes.

"I mean, I know we're not being overheard *now*," he said, in a strangely louder voice. One of the eyes closed in a broad wink. His arms had been folded across his chest, and suddenly the thumb of the right hand stirred and began to wag slowly in the direction of the bushes behind him. "I do know *that*," he said (with the wink seeming to add, "In a pig's eye!"). "But all the same, you should be more careful."

They were all alert now, watching Joe's face, ready for a command. Danny fancied he heard the catch of someone's breath—not quite a gasp but audible enough—up in the bushes. But before he could think about it any further, Joe had leaped to his feet.

"*Quick! Get 'em!*" he yelled.

They knew what to do, now that the time had come. Joe had made this quite clear, earlier.

"They may stick together or they may split up," he had said. "In any case, I want you, Karen, to go after the girl. Danny can back you up. Carlos and I will concentrate on the boy."

"But why?" Karen had protested. "He's likely to run faster than her, and I'm the fastest runner of us all."

"I know that. But you're a girl, and she's a girl. So you won't be too likely to get squeamish if you have to subdue her when you've grabbed her. She looks like she could be a real handful."

"Yes, well, that's true, but—"

"And also it's more important to make sure of *her*. No matter how fast he is, when he sees she's been collared, he'll give himself up. He looks the type. Responsible. More anxious for her safety than his own."

So that was the plan they followed when Joe yelled the command and the kids burst from the bushes and, in their panic, the boy went running one way and the girl raced off in another.

Joe and Carlos lit out after the boy, who was making for the nearest stretch of woodland; Karen and Danny went after the girl, who headed for more of the open grassy area. And in this, whether by chance or instinct, the boy had made the better choice.

For catching a ghost among trees is not easy, even when the chaser is another ghost. There is no help to be had for the chaser from such hazards as large surface roots or fallen branches, which might trip up a living person. The branches and roots may be there, all right, and a ghost's feet and legs certainly wouldn't be able to go straight *through* these obstacles, any easier than a ghost could go through a solid wall.

But a ghost's special instincts and reflexes seem to take care of such minor stumbling hazards, causing him to run up and over a log or between any raised-up roots at the last split second, even when he's failed to see them in time, even on the darkest night. It is as if there were some batlike radar system in operation.

This radar, however, doesn't operate when other ghostly bodies are the obstacles. Let a ghost be lying down in the long grass and another ghost come speeding toward him unwittingly, then nothing on earth can save that speeding ghost from taking a dive over the body of the other ghost. Then it's as if the runner had been a living person and the body a log.

And that's what happened that night.

The girl was fast—faster than Karen and Danny had expected. And she'd had a few seconds' start, with fear acting as an extra boost. Danny soon found himself falling behind, while Karen was unable at first to notice any shortening of the distance between her and the small fleeing figure, whose white socks continued to be a blur in the darkness ahead.

But she needn't have worried.

A little farther on, the very serious ghost of a man was lying on his back, looking up at the stars. They never found out who he was, but probably—like many of the ghosts in that neighborhood—he had had a very distinguished career in life. Possibly he'd even come close to being prime minister of the United Kingdom and was in the habit of strolling on the heath every evening to gaze down on the capital of the country he might easily have been the leader of. And possibly, on this particular evening, after pondering over what a mess things were in down there and how *he* could have done so much to improve matters if he'd been spared, he flung himself down on the grass to think things over and sigh for what might have been.

Anyway, whoever or whatever he had been, it was over him that Samantha took an almighty tumble.

"Gotcha!" said Karen, pouncing on her sprawling body.

"Terrific!" gasped Danny, just arriving.

"Hooligans!" growled the distinguished-looking ghost, getting up and stalking away. "Girls, too! It would never have got to this had I had *my* way!"

But Karen, Samantha and Danny were paying no attention. Samantha was too busy trying to break loose, and Karen was too busy trying to keep Samantha's clawing hands from doing a much nastier and more lasting corrugating job on her face than ever the supersonic flight could have done.

"Her hands, Danny! Grab her hands! Don't just stand there!"

It was easier said than done. Samantha was struggling like a wildcat, spitting and scratching and snarling. And things might have gone very badly for Karen's and Danny's features (for ghosts can do all the damage to other ghosts that living persons can do to each other), if another voice hadn't made itself heard.

"Samantha! Please! They don't mean us any harm, I'm sure!"

It was Bernard, flanked by Joe and Carlos. They weren't even holding him by now. It was just as Joe had figured. The boy's anxiety and concern for his sister had been more powerful than any physical force.

Samantha's body stiffened and froze.

Then she went limp.

"All right," she muttered. "If you're sure—"

"I *am* sure," said Bernard, glancing uneasily at Joe despite the confidence in his tone.

Joe nodded and gave the boy's shoulder a reassuring pat.

"You can be sure," he said gently. "*We're* out to nail Jackman, too."

At these words, the girl sat up, alert but relaxed.

"You *are?*" she said. Then, as Joe nodded, she turned to Karen and Danny. "I'm sorry," she said quickly. "Did I hurt you?"

They shook their heads.

"Huh-uh!" said Danny, trying to grin through the spasms of pain that still came and went in the groin area, where one of Samantha's flying feet had caught him.

"Not at all, honey," said Karen, sighing with relief to find no blood on her fingers after their quick exploration of her right cheek.

Then, in the grassy hollow vacated by the distinguished ghost, they all sat around and gave an account of their connections with Jackman.

The American ghosts gave their report first, telling the others how Danny and Carlos had encountered Jackman with Danny's mother in the Lakeview Hotel restaurant, of their suspicions about the man and of how they'd followed him into the room and overheard his conversation with the other man. Then, omitting completely any mention of Buzz and Wacko—in line with Joe's earlier warning—they went on to describe their decision to investigate closer, and their Concorde flight earlier in the day.

Joe did most of the talking, allowing Danny and Carlos only to fill in with firsthand descriptions of what they'd seen and heard at the Lakeview Hotel. Even then, he kept a very sharp eye on the two boys, especially Carlos, ready to interrupt at the first hint of any talk about the word processor and their living colleagues.

He needn't have worried. The only interruptions came from the British pair.

Much of the time, Samantha and Bernard listened in silence, intently, merely murmuring their agreement now and then, or—when Jackman's phone call was mentioned—looking at each other and nodding.

"That would be Turner," Bernard said.

"Yes—another horrible man!" Samantha replied, her eyes flashing.

Her eyes flashed a lot as the others' narrative continued, especially when Jackman was physically described. But at the end, when Joe said, "And that's it. Here we are. You know the rest—" she swung her head toward Danny, and the flashing was replaced by a steady burning.

"You were so right! So right to feel that your mother and sisters and brothers are in danger. They are! That man"—she seemed to gag at the thought of speaking his name—"that—that *monster*—killed our mother! And us!"

"Well, Sam, I wouldn't—"

"He did, he did, he did!" Samantha nearly screamed the words. Her eyes still burned, even though they were now brimming over with tears. Danny, sitting next to her, wouldn't have been surprised to see steam rising from them. "He killed us *all!*"

The Americans looked uneasy, glancing from sister to brother and back again.

"Take it easy, Sam," said Bernard, softly. "You're quite right. But let *me* tell them about it."

Samantha nodded, shuddered and hung her head so

that her hair fell over her face. Then she remained silent while her brother began their story.

It was not a pleasant one.

Jackman had been their stepfather.

Their natural father, the original owner of the store, had died years ago, not long after Samantha was born. It had been a thriving business, and for some years it had continued to do well under their mother's ownership. She had not been as knowledgeable about antiques as her husband, but she'd received a lot of help from other dealers, who'd all admired and respected him. In fact, if it hadn't been for their support, she might have gone to pieces quite soon.

"Mummy always had been rather weak in times of difficulty," Bernard went on, looking anxiously at his sister.

The hanging hair shook.

"It's all right, Bernard. Tell them. They should know this."

"Well—"

"Mummy used to drink!" she said, looking up and glaring at them defiantly. Then her eyes softened as they rested on Danny. "Like—like yours."

"Well, anyway," Bernard hurried on, "she never had any serious problem until Jackman came along. And at first that went smoothly, too. . . ."

Jackman had appeared about two and a half years previously. He had first met their mother when he entered the shop as a customer, but both Bernard and Samantha were convinced that he'd spent quite a number of weeks beforehand casing the place, finding out all he could about the widow and how well the business was doing. And, of course, once he'd become friendly with her, his pitch was as smooth and disarming as it had been with Danny's mother.

"Same approach, too," said Bernard. "He told *our* mother he was independently wealthy. That he had a large amount of property, farms and millions of dollars' worth of timber, in the States. Family property, he said it was—close to his hometown."

"That's a lie anyway!" said Karen.

"Yes. *We* know that now," said Bernard. "But he backed this pitch up with documents, too. Forgeries, obviously."

"It's his standard MO," Joe said. "That's for sure."

Then—more hesitantly now—Bernard continued his narrative. How his mother had fallen for Jackman's stories. How they'd married. How the sweetness—the honey and syrup—had continued to be poured over her for another month or so. And then the change.

"He started taking over the business. He called it helping her at first. But she noticed things. Like money being drawn out of their joint account—oh, yes! She was foolish enough to open one with him. He has a very persuasive tongue, our stepfather. He—"

"*Don't call him that!*" rasped Samantha, in a voice that made them all look scared. "*I hate him!*"

Bernard sighed and continued—speeding up his narrative, trying to make it as unemotional as possible as he told them of other things Jackman had done without their mother's knowledge or consent: shifty deals on the side, where he had bought articles of very doubtful value and sold them at exorbitant prices, counting on the good name of the business to lull the unsuspecting buyers.

And then their mother had become angry—and

Jackman had shown his real character. There were violent arguments. She started drinking more. He kept up the pressure, deliberately provoking her. He was nasty with the kids. He began to do and say things in their presence that disgusted them all. Their mother's nerves became shot. Her drinking increased still more.

"Then he brought in Turner. Fred Turner."

"Another beast!"

"He claimed to be expert in the trade, but it soon became clear that he was just an old crony of Jackman's. Someone he'd probably shared a cell with or something. At any rate, he knew nothing at all about antiques, except maybe the best places to fence stolen ones. *And he moved in with us.*"

There was a silence for a few minutes, broken only by Samantha's sobs.

"Go on, Bern!" she said at last. "Go—get it over with!"

Just over ten months before the meeting of the six ghosts, there had been a terrific fight at the Jackman residence. Other undesirable characters had started dropping in, and their mother was reaching her breaking point. On that evening, the kids had been all set to go to a friend's birthday party, but Mrs. Jackman, already three-parts drunk and in a state of almost hysterical distress, had bundled them into the car and announced to Jackman and Turner that they wouldn't be coming back.

Jackman had sneered. Turner had grinned.

"And that must have been it. She didn't say another word until we we were out in the country. Up until then, her driving had been fairly steady, considering. We just kept quiet, hoping she knew where she was going. Then, all at once, something must have snapped. She yelled something about not being able to stand it any longer, put her foot down—and steered deliberately into a telephone pole at eighty-five miles an hour."

They all looked at Samantha. Her head was hanging again. She was crouched, huddled up, her knees to her chest. She was sobbing steadily.

"The rest you can almost guess," said Bernard. "Jackman had at last got complete control of the business. But it didn't do him much good. Since we've—uh—been able to look in on him, at least we've had the satisfaction of noting *that*. His greed got worse. He took far more money out of the shop than ever came in. Other dealers very quickly began to give him the cold shoulder. He had to make deals that were shadier and shadier. Even Turner has started to get worried. And now Jackman is so desperate he's had to fall back on this buried treasure business."

"So he says!" murmured Joe.

"No. He is genuinely hooked on it. Something about some hoard of gold sovereigns hidden in a cellar, somewhere back near his hometown. We watched him poring over the map one evening."

"Yeah—but his real business at the moment is more connected with his *regular* MO," Joe said, casting a glance at Danny. "He—"

Then Samantha cut loose. With tears streaming down her face, she lifted her head and cried out, as if to the stars:

"Nothing can bring us back together with Mummy!

Nothing! Nothing! Nothing! Because—because she killed herself and su-suicides never—never—*ever* become ghosts!"

She was trembling all over. Bernard looked scared.

Joe took a deep breath and went across to her, crouching in front of her. He gently took her hands in his.

"Listen, honey," he said, "listen to me, please. I've been a ghost longer than you, longer than any of those here now. And I know that people who—who commit suicide don't come back as regular ghosts, like us. But who's to say there aren't other kinds of ghosts, at other levels, and that your mom isn't here right now, listening to you, wanting to help—the way *we* do with people still living?"

"But—but—"

"Listen, honey. When you were alive, *you* didn't believe in ghosts, right? Ghosts like us?"

"No—but—"

"Well, then, how can we be so sure, now, that there aren't these other ghosts—this other level of ghosts—watching us and listening to us? And maybe looking forward to when we'll be joining them?"

"Oh—do you *really* think so?"

The little girl's eyes were shining with a more human, hopeful light.

"I do, honey."

The girl sighed, then nodded.

"Thank you," she said softly. Then, turning to her brother, she said, "But I still think *Jackman* killed her. And us. By making her so—so . . . by driving her to do what she did!"

"Sure," said Karen, putting an arm around her. "I'm sure you're right about that."

"And anyway," Samantha went on, getting fierce again, "he *is* a murderer! And—"

"Yes," said Bernard, "but let's get down to business, Sam. We all want to nail Jackman. If we *can*."

He looked at Joe.

"Right!" said Joe. "And we're counting on your help. *Can* you help us?" he added, repeating Bernard's emphasis.

"Yes!" said Samantha, firmly.

"Possibly," said Bernard. He thought for a few moments. Then: "Look—can you be outside the shop tomorrow morning at ten, when it opens for business? Ready to slip inside as soon as the door is opened?"

"Sure!" said Joe. "We were planning to do just that."

"Good!" said Bernard. "Then we'll meet you there. Come on, Sam, we have work to do, remember? And we don't want to leave it too late."

And, without another word, the British pair got up and left.

"I wonder what the work is that he was talking about?" said Carlos.

"I don't know," said Joe. "He seemed to be in too much of a hurry to explain. But that's OK. I have a hunch we'll find out soon."

"What I'd like to know," said Karen, after a while, "is if there *is* any truth in that buried treasure story."

"Yeah!" said Carlos. "Me, too! And if Buzz and Wacko have found out anything about it yet!"

12

Buzz and Wacko Advertise for Temporary Summer Help

It had been a beautiful day in the Ghost Squad's hometown, with a sunset to match. Not that there was any majestic vista for Buzz and Wacko to look down upon from where *they* sat—once again on a parking lot guardrail outside the station. They couldn't even see the sun from there, because it had already sunk below the roofs of the buildings across the street.

But the air itself seemed stained by its color—a deep rose that got deeper by the minute, dusting over the outlines of the buildings and turning the shadows a soft purple.

The two boys weren't in much of a mood to appreciate this, however. They were feeling tired and more than a little dissatisfied. They had been hanging around that spot for hours, and the rented station wagon had only just returned. Mrs. Green, Jackman and the kids had gone straight into the house, and it was beginning to look like that was it for the day.

"But they can't have been up Sentinel Mountain prodding around for root cellars all this time, surely!" said Buzz.

"I wouldn't know," said Wacko, stifling a yawn. "Maybe we should have stayed and seen for ourselves."

Buzz shook his head firmly.

"Too risky. If Jackman had spotted us spying on him up there, that would have blown everything. My guess is that he's very touchy about that treasure."

"Yeah. But still—I never figured they'd be all this time. I—hey! Here's Mike and Jilly now!"

It was like a replica of the morning scene, this time in deep rose and dusky purple instead of blue and gold. The kids were turning the corner with the shopping cart. The boys crossed over quickly.

"Hi, Mike! Hi, Jilly!"

They both looked tired and disheveled. They seemed more disposed to lean on the cart's handle than tug at it.

"Oh . . . hi!" said Mike.

"Don't tell me you're shopping for another picnic?"

"*No!*" said Jilly scornfully, grinning at Buzz as if she thought he was some dummy who needed humoring.

"Just supper stuff," said Mike.

"You look bushed, the pair of you. How did the treasure hunt go?"

"Oh—*that!*" Mike shrugged. "There wasn't any."

"We gave up on it," said Jilly.

"I bet Mr. Jackman was mad, wasn't he?"

Mike shrugged again.

"Some. I guess."

"Not really, though," said Jilly. "Only right at the start."

"He's OK really," said Mike. "I guess."

"He took us for *treats*," said Jilly, widening her pale blue eyes. "He took us to a McDonald's and let us order whatever we wanted. And then he took us to an old village place where all the folks was dressed up like old history folks."

"Yeah!" said Mike, catching some of her enthusiasm. "And we watched this guy in a funny hat shoeing horses—"

"And a lady in a long dress and big white cap with frills and ribbons and stuff was making taffy, and she let us all try some, and Arnie ate so much he got sick."

"Sounds terrific," murmured Wacko.

"Yeah!" said Jilly, taking his comment seriously. "It was!"

"But didn't Mr. Jackman get mad at *all*, after you'd stopped looking for the treasure?" said Buzz. "I mean like later, maybe? Like when Arnie was sick?"

Jilly giggled.

"Oh, it wasn't in the *car* he threw up! It was before we got back to it. And all Mr. Jaxman said then was it served Arnie right for being a pig. Only he was laughing when he said it."

"He's all right, I guess," Mike murmured.

"The only time he did get a *little* mad," said Jilly, "just an itty bit, was coming home in the car, and Sylvia kept saying she felt cold, that it was cold way in back where she was."

"But it wasn't really," said Mike. "I was back there, too, and—"

"And Mr. Jaxman turned the air condi—condisher thing—off, and she still kept saying she felt cold. And then he got a little mad and said maybe *she* ate too much taffy too and she better not be sick in the car."

"But she wasn't," said Mike. "And she stopped feeling cold. So that was OK. I guess Mr.—"

"Hey, you two! You gonna take all night?"

More than Mike jumped, then.

It was Jackman, at the corner, glaring at them.

"No, sir!" said Mike. "Sorry!" He glanced up at Buzz. "We gotta go now. . . ."

"And hurry it up!" said Jackman. "And—hey!—get a pack of Alka-Seltzer while you're there. Your mom's not feeling too good."

When the kids had gone creaking on their way, the man walked up to Buzz and Wacko, peering at them in a manner that was either shortsighted or suspicious.

"Aren't you the two guys who were up in the hills, talking to Mike?"

Suspicious, Buzz decided. Definitely. Definitely ug-*lee*.

"Yes—we—uh—"

"You friends of his or something?"

The skin on the forehead and under that wiglike fuzz of sandy hair looked inflamed and irritated, already peeling in places. The man's temper seemed to be just as frayed.

"I said, are you friends of his?"

"Well, sort of," Buzz began. "We—"

The man's mouth had bunched up into a soft but very nasty sneer.

"Kind of old to be hanging around young kids, aren't you?"

Buzz flushed.

"What's that supposed to mean?"

"Don't 'that-supposed-to-mean' *me*, sonny! You know what I mean. Young kids, with more money than sense, and no man around the house to look out for them—they sort of get taken by older kids, out for easy pickings. Know what I mean?"

What stung Buzz most was the leer on Jackman's face. Like it was OK by him, that sort of thing, so long as they went and did it to some *other* young kids. Like he was judging Buzz and Wacko by his own standards, lumping them in with *him*, for Pete's sake!

"That's a dirty—"

Wacko tugged at Buzz's sleeve. Hard.

"Come on, Buzz. Let's go."

"Yeah!" sneered Jackman. "You better! Because if I catch you hanging around those kids again, there'll be trouble!"

Then he turned and went back.

"Wow!" gasped Buzz, when Wacko had steered him back across the street. "*Phew-wee!* Can you *believe* that guy? The—the *nerve* of him? Accusing us of doing on a small scale exactly what *he's* doing on—on—"

"Cool it, Buzz. Cool it. Sit down a minute on this rail. Come on. Sit. Sit. . . . Remember, we have a job to do."

Buzz took a deep breath of the hot, polluted, rose-colored air. It didn't do much for him in the way of cooling his anger. But he had to agree with Wacko.

"Yeah," he murmured. "I know. But there's something else . . . I mean, how can we do that job *now?* You can be sure Jackman'll put the fear of God into those kids about us, from now on. I mean, who knows what kind of lies he'll be telling them about us?"

Wacko grunted.

"We'll just have to be more careful, that's all."

"Yeah. . . . But—oh—if only one of the others *had* stayed behind!" He'd raised his head in anguish at this point, as if pleading with some Being up above, in the darkening sky. Then he grinned shyly—aware of how melodramatic he must have sounded. "No, though—what we really need is some temporary help. Some spare ghost to fill in while the others are enjoying themselves over in London. Some temporary summer help."

Wacko grinned, wistfully.

"Sure! But where would we advertise? We can't put a notice on the supermarket bulletin board: *Wanted— keen, reliable ghost for summer job. Must be willing to work all hours, day and night.*"

Buzz laughed. Gradually, he was beginning to feel much less uptight.

"No!" he said. "Bulletin board nothing! Where've you been these last few weeks, Wacko? All we'd have to do is stand around someplace—any place—right here—and say out loud: 'If any ghost is listening and would like a job, please touch my right ear!' "

He stood up for this, suiting his action to the words. But he had no sooner uttered the last of those words than a look of massive shock struck his face, and he clapped a hand to his right ear.

Wacko smiled up at him, uncertainly.

"Hey, come *on*, Buzz! Quit fooling! You gave me quite a fright for a second there!"

Buzz's mouth was half-open. It began to move—hesitantly at first. Then:

"No—I—I *wasn't* fooling. I—I'm sure I—"

He blinked, frowned. His face took on a look of fierce concentration as he stared into the thickening space, now turning from rose to dusky crimson.

"Listen!" he said, still staring in front of him. "If there really is a ghost present—touch my nose. And *his*."

Buzz felt the touch. A faint cool brush, as of a fly's wing. Right on the tip of his nose.

There was a crashing at the side of him. Wacko was scrambling to his feet after falling off the guardrail. His eyes were popping with awe as they stared up at Buzz, over the hand that he'd clapped to his nose. There was no need for him to say a word.

Wacko too had felt that ghostly touch!

13
The Applicant

The boys just stared at each other for several seconds. All around them, the life of the town was proceeding as usual. A train rumbled into the station. Somebody started a car in the lot behind them. Pedestrians passed them by on the sidewalk, close to where their new acquaintance had to be standing. Lights began to show up brighter in the gathering dusk. A plane droned above them.

Then Buzz gave a start, and a feeble, rather shaky grin began to spread across his face.

"Hey!" he drawled, turning his head from side to side as if he were addressing a small group of people. "Come *on*, you guys! It *is* you, isn't it? Or one of you?"

By now, Wacko was beginning to smile too—realizing what Buzz was getting at.

"What happened?" Buzz continued, still addressing

empty space. "Did you miss the plane or something?"

He stiffened slightly, prepared to acknowledge the faint touch he expected on one of his ears.

There was no reply. He guessed he'd been asking too many questions all at once. Wacko must have been thinking the same.

"Take it more slowly, Buzz. One question at a time."

Buzz nodded.

"OK. Is it Carlos?"

No touch, no faint flicker of coolness, nothing.

Buzz frowned.

"Is it Danny, then?"

Again, nothing.

Buzz had lost some of his confidence by now. Surely, if it had been another member of the squad, wouldn't he or she have answered by touching his *left* ear?

He pressed on, asking if it were Karen, and then Joe—with the same result.

"Nothing," he murmured, turning to Wacko.

Wacko gulped.

"Maybe—maybe we just imagined it earlier. Maybe—*yeek!*"

He'd clapped his hand over his nose again.

Then Buzz felt a touch on *his* nose. In fact, he felt a series of touches: one-two-three-four, in quick succession.

He cleared his throat and cast a scared glance at Wacko.

"It looks like we've attracted a new one," he said.

"Yeah, I suppose—I suppose we'd better follow through—now we—now it's started. Huh?"

Buzz nodded. He took a deep breath.

"Yes. Why not? OK—uh—you—whoever you are . . ."

What followed was one of the shortest—and certainly the strangest—job interviews of all time.

"First," said Buzz, keeping his voice low, hoping that any passersby who heard him would think he was talking to Wacko while idly watching the traffic at the same time—"first of all, you'd better understand the code. When I ask a question, you answer by touching my left ear for no or my right ear for yes. Do you understand?"

A fly seemed to alight on his right ear. The coolness lingered there for two or three seconds.

"All right, all right!" said Buzz. "One quick touch is enough. There's no need to *shout!*"

Had it been one of the Ghost Squad he was addressing, Wacko might have grinned at Buzz's exasperated comment. But this was much too serious.

"Go on, Buzz," he muttered. "Get on with the questions."

Buzz nodded. He turned to the front again.

"OK. So tell me this. Are you fooling or do you really want to work for us?"

This time the response was on both ears—left, right—in quick succession.

Buzz blinked.

"Sorry!" he said. "I keep forgetting. One thing at a time. Now—do you really want to work for us?"

This time he got two on his right ear.

He blinked again. Was that meant for emphasis? Or—

"Hey! Are there *two* of you?"

Left ear.

Buzz sighed with relief. One stranger ghost was bad enough. A bunch of them would have been *too* much.

"Well, anyway," he went on, "what we want to know about is if a guy called Jackman—"

A touch on his right ear interrupted him. Another lingering one.

"You know him, then?"

Right ear.

"Good!" Buzz was beginning to warm to his task. "Well, first we want to know if he's really serious about some buried treasure, up in—"

Right ear.

"You know about that already?"

Right ear.

Buzz looked at Wacko and nodded, his eyes wide.

"Ask him—ask him, has Jackman found it yet?"

This time both boys received a reply. Both on the left ear.

"Is Jackman *close* to finding it?" Wacko asked.

No reply.

The boys looked at each other, questioningly. Both shook their heads.

"Does that mean you don't know? Touch my left ear if you don't," Buzz added hastily, anticipating complications.

The newcomer touched Buzz's left ear.

"But you *will* keep us informed?"

Right ear.

"And more important than the treasure—we'd like to know—we *have* to know—if he makes any definite arrangements to marry a lady called Mrs. Green. Do you know who—?"

Right ear.

100

"Good. Well, we're not just prying. This is on a need-to-know basis. Uh—it's very important—and—" (Right ear.) "I mean, we think the man is a crook and a swindler, a nasty cheating rogue and—"

Buzz broke off. His right ear had been touched three times. It was as if the invisible applicant were saying: "You bet he is! You can't tell me anything about that guy I don't already know!"

Buzz was beginning to feel they'd made a lucky strike. This seemed like a helper with his heart and soul in the job. Just what they wanted.

"OK. So if Jackman does try to rush her into a quick marriage, we must know in plenty of time. Is that clear?"

Right ear.

"Good—well—so we can leave it to you to find out what you can?"

Right ear.

"And you know where Mrs. Green lives, just over—?"

Right ear. The new help seemed to be impatient to start work.

"Fine!" said Buzz, looking at Wacko and giving him the thumbs-up sign. "Great! So—uh—why don't we meet here, this same spot, tomorrow morning, and get your first report? Say—uh"—he glanced at Wacko again—"nine o'clock?"

Wacko nodded. The invisible helper touched Buzz's right ear.

"Good. So that's settled then?"

No reply.

"Are you still here?"

No reply.

"*Are* you still here?"

Again no reply.

Buzz turned to Wacko.

"He must have gotten straight onto the job." He grinned. "I have to say he seems very alert and eager, whoever he—or she—is."

Wacko was frowning slightly.

"I wonder, though, if—"

"Hey, don't look so worried, Wacko! I mean—come on—it's just the sort of help we need. I mean we shouldn't look a gift horse in the mouth. And that goes for gift *ghosts*, too."

Wacko smiled, still uneasy, but more relaxed.

"No. Maybe not. But I'd feel a whole lot better if we could look him in the *eyes*."

"Forget it! The others'll do that for us, when they get back."

Wacko's grin faded.

"Yeah—*when!* They haven't been gone a whole day yet."

"Well, whenever. Meantime we can at least *ask* this one tomorrow. Like if he's a *he* or a *she*, old or young, and so on. Sort of get more acquainted."

Wacko still wasn't looking too happy.

Then he shrugged.

"Oh, well—we're stuck with him now, I guess. We might as well make the best use of him we can."

"Now," said Buzz, slapping him on the shoulder, "you're talking!"

And with that, they decided to call it a day.

14
The Haunted Man

By 10 A.M. next morning—while it was only 5 A.M. in the eastern United States and Buzz and Wacko were still sleeping uneasily—the rest of the Ghost Squad was waiting outside the antique store.

It was another twenty minutes, however, before the CLOSED card was reversed and the door was opened from the inside. During the wait, the ghosts had started getting fidgety—but they needn't have worried. From that point on, they were in luck.

The morning was sunny and quite hot by British standards, and the man who stepped out onto the doorstep was in no hurry to get back inside. He stood for a while taking deep breaths and glancing up and down the street. The ghosts had as much time as they needed to slip past him into the store.

"He *looks* like he needs some air!" said Karen.

He was a tall, thin man with a pale face and staring

eyes that had dark blue pouches of wrinkled flesh under them. His head was bald on top, but the remaining hair and long sideburns were still a dusty brown color. His bony chin and cheeks also had a blue cast, matching the flesh under his eyes—though this was not because he hadn't shaved that morning, judging from the two still glistening cuts, one on his upper lip and the other on the side of his jaw. He was wearing a gray suit, well cut and obviously expensive, but it needed pressing and looked as if it had been put on hastily, as if he'd been in a hurry to get somewhere—or leave somewhere. His red silk necktie had obviously been knotted hurriedly, overtightly. Already he had tugged it out of place and opened the top button of his shirt, releasing a large restless Adam's apple that seemed to have permanent goose bumps.

"I bet he's Jackman's partner," said Carlos.

They watched him as, with a sigh that was almost a groan, the man closed the door and shuffled to a desk that faced it. There was a cup of coffee on a small silver tray and a newspaper roughly folded at the crossword puzzle. His hand, hairy and spidery, shook as he lifted the cup to his lips and his eyes ranged restlessly, this way and that, over the rim. He seemed to be vaguely conscious of the fact that something was not right. Something very unnatural.

"It's like he can *sense* someone else is here," said Danny.

"*We hope so!*"

The ghosts turned, startled.

It was Bernard and Samantha, just entering through an open doorway leading to another part of the store.

"I see you're making the acquaintance of Mr. Fred Turner," said Bernard, grinning.

Joe glanced at the street door. It was firmly closed.

"Hey!" he said. "When did *you* get in?"

"Last night," said Samantha. "Just after we'd left you. We've been keeping him company practically every night for the last few weeks."

"We were afraid we might have missed him last night," said Bernard. "He stays out as late as he can. But last night, of course, we were late too."

"But we were just in time," said Samantha, smiling at the other ghosts but with a glint in her eye whenever she glanced at the man.

"So we kept him company," said Bernard.

The other ghosts were puzzled.

"But—what's so attractive about *him?*" said Karen.

The man had just taken a slurp of his cool scummy-looking coffee. His hand must have shaken so much at that moment that some of the coffee dribbled down his chin and onto his tie. But he seemed to be beyond caring about trifles like that. He simply brushed his chin with the back of his hand and went on staring at the crossword puzzle, as if trying to fix his eyes on something—anything—to keep them from roving around in that frightened way.

"His nerves," said Samantha, staring at him with loathing. "That's what's so attractive about him. The *only* thing."

"He's a very nervous man, as you can see," said Bernard, giving his sister an uneasy glance. "And we're trying to break him down. . . . Samantha! No!"

But the girl was already at Turner's side, bending

over his coffee cup. Her face was twisted with hate. She tried to spit into the cup—but the spittle, real enough for a ghost, never got further than her lips. Whatever of it left them simply disappeared instantly, leaving only a light froth on her lower lip.

The attempt had a look of such intense viciousness that more than one of the others found themselves shuddering.

"Cut it out, Sam!" snapped Bernard. "You know it's a waste of energy!"

Samantha hovered there, still staring at the man. Then she gave her head a brisk shake and, with a forced unsteady smile, went back to her brother's side.

"Sorry!" she mumbled. "I—I just lose control—sometimes."

"You were saying about trying to break him down," Joe said to Bernard. "Not like that, I hope?"

"No . . . no. And I did say 'trying.' It's not been too successful so far, I admit. But it's the best we can do."

"*I* wouldn't say you hadn't been successful," murmured Karen, staring at the continually bobbing Adam's apple and the dark flesh under the man's eyes.

"No. But we still seem to be a long way short of making him crack completely," said Bernard. "I mean really crack. So that he'll go running to the police and tell them everything."

"And so fix Jackman," said Samantha. "For good!"

"But how?" said Joe. "The poltergeist method?"

"The what?" said Samantha, looking up eagerly.

"Getting delicately balanced objects to suddenly crash down, for no reason at all," said Joe. "Things like that."

"Well—no," murmured Bernard, looking interested. "No. I haven't heard of that."

"*We* try to get him in his dreams!" said Samantha.

"You do?" said Carlos. "Hey, come on! That's next to impossible!"

Bernard sighed.

"I know. It certainly isn't easy. In fact, it's only remotely possible because of the *way* he sometimes dreams."

"You don't mean getting at him through his own temporary ghost, do you?" said Danny. "Is that it?"

"Yes," said Bernard. "You know it then? Have *you* ever been successful?"

"Only once," said Danny, shaking his head. "With a friend of mine." He turned to his colleagues. "Buzz Phillips, remember?" He turned back to Bernard and Samantha. "But it was only to wake him up in an emergency. Which I did."

Danny went on to explain how Buzz had been having that special sort of dream when a person dreams of himself sleeping. "Like he is still in the same room, watching himself sleeping. Which is exactly what he *is* doing, because his own ghost, his 'astral body' as Joe calls it—right, Joe?—it steps out of the shell of his living body for a short distance. Just like an astronaut going for a walk in space."

"Yes, yes!" cried Samantha, clapping her hands. "That's just what *he* does."

"Yes," said Bernard, more soberly. "Fortunately, Chummy here often sleeps like that. I think it's the sleeping pills he takes. Plus whatever he's had to drink in the evening. Of course, it doesn't *always* act like that. But—"

"But when it does, we haunt him through his own mangy ghost!" said Samantha. "Which *can* hear us and see us!"

Joe was looking very interested.

"And does it work?"

Samantha's eager smile faded. Bernard shrugged.

"Not very well, I'm afraid."

"The trouble is," said Samantha, "as soon as his ghost sees us, it shrinks back into his body. Like—like a rat back into its hole."

"Yes," said Bernard. "So now we're experimenting with just talking to it, without letting it actually see us."

"We hide behind the curtains and things, like we were all three living people."

"What do you say?" asked Karen.

"Oh, things like we know what he's done," said Bernard. "And why doesn't he confess to the police and get it off his chest."

Samantha's lip curled.

"But even then, even when he can't see us, he soon starts shrinking back into his grotty body again!"

"And we're not even sure he remembers any of it when he awakes."

"No," said Samantha. "Except we can see that it's *disturbed* him. Look at him now."

Turner was fidgeting with his pen. He hadn't been able to fill in a single blank square of his crossword puzzle. He was staring at the black-and-white checkered pattern but didn't seem to be seeing it at all.

Carlos was seething with excitement.

"Hey, well, we have news for you! You say you

aren't even sure he remembers anything you say or do. Well—"

"*Carlos!*"

The instant Joe spoke, Carlos remembered.

Never—ever—to disclose their secret to any other ghost.

And in telling Bernard and Samantha once again about what he and Danny had overheard in the Lakeview Hotel room—this time in greater detail—Carlos could easily get carried away and spill something about their connection with Buzz and Wacko.

He nodded. Message received. He proceeded more cautiously.

"Well, when I was telling you last night about overhearing what he was saying to Jackman on the phone, I didn't mention he said something about bad dreams."

"And thinking he was being haunted by some kids," said Danny.

"Really?" said Bernard.

"*Oh, Danny, you've made my day!*" sang Samantha, darting over and giving Danny a big hug. "I don't think you look at all scruffy, really, and—"

"Samantha!"

Bernard obviously had some of the same problems as Joe, when it came to the overeagerness of partners.

"Anyway," said Joe, still not happy about where all the excitement might lead, especially when Samantha went and hugged Carlos too, "anyway, let me tell you more about the poltergeist method. Maybe give you a demonstration. If you'll just take us on a tour of the store, I'll see if I can spot any likely subjects . . ."

There were several showrooms, and the doors to all of them had been left wide open to give easy access to any customer who might come in and wish to browse. No doubt if that had happened, Turner would have abandoned his crossword puzzle, ready to answer questions and generally keep an eye on the visitor or visitors. But no customer did come in just then, and the six visitors who went prowling around the store were quite invisible to him.

Which—for the sake of his nerves—was just as well, because never had a party of keen antiques collectors given the objects on display a closer, more sinister scrutiny. Bulky pieces of furniture, large oil paintings and heavy candlesticks were passed over without much comment. But small items—figurines, finely painted plates propped on shelves, small colored glasses, a group of Victorian dolls that had been made to stand up in a circle, holding each others' hands, on a small round table—items like that caused the visitors to pause and stoop and hold long murmured discussions.

To a man like Turner, himself a crook, it would have suggested one thing only: shoplifters. Shoplifters operating in a gang and waiting for the chance to pocket such costly objects.

But he continued to sit at the desk, twitching his pen, oblivious to the excited cry of Carlos on spotting the ring of dolls in the next room.

"Hey! How about these? They look like they're all supporting each other by their own weight; their feet aren't flat enough to balance on their own."

"Yeah," Joe grunted, crouching to get a better look. "One falls, they all fall. Just one quick prod at that sailor boy would do it."

110

"So do it, Joe! Do it! Do it!"

Samantha was clapping her hands again.

But as he straightened up, Joe shook his head.

"Delicately balanced, yes. But not delicately enough for us, I'm afraid."

"Oh, come out of the way!" said Samantha, pushing Joe aside and giving the sailor doll a clip with the back of her hand.

Joe felt the force of her thrust. Husky as he was, he was caught off-balance and blundered into Danny.

But the fragile wax doll didn't budge a hair's breadth. The vicious slap just seemed to slide off the side of its head.

"That isn't the way to do it anyway, honey," said Karen, putting a gentle calming hand on Samantha's shoulder. "A ghost has to concentrate. Sort of *channel* his energy. Through his fingertips and the pores of his skin. That's if he wants to make any difference to solid objects, no matter how delicately balanced."

"Sorry!" murmured Samantha.

"That's OK," said Joe, passing on to a row of fine china figurines ranged along a narrow shelf—tiny shepherdesses and bowing young swains, holding their cocked hats in one hand and seeming to balance on one leg, with only the tips of the toes of the bending leg touching the ground. "Now these I might have been able to do something with. If only the guy had been more careless and placed them nearer the edge."

"Not much chance of that!" said Bernard, wincing. "He may be bad, he may be jittery. But with the price tag that *they* have, he'd never be so careless."

"No," said Samantha. "They're genuine Dresden. Even I wouldn't like to see *them* fall off."

111

And that seemed to be the one big problem. The high cost of most of the articles in that store almost automatically ensured that they would never have been left in precarious positions. A proud housewife in her own home couldn't have handled such treasures more carefully than the two ruffians to whom they represented much-needed profit.

Only after about an hour's careful searching did Joe come up with something both suitable and cheap, and even then it was Turner himself who pointed it out.

"Damn!" they heard him yelp from the next room. "Get away!"

They hurried in, wondering if he'd flipped after all. But it was only a fly—a large bluebottle—that had been bothering him.

They watched as Turner stalked it with the folded newspaper. It lit on a fine old chest.

"He'll never swipe at it there, mad as he is," Bernard predicted. "That's a genuine Chippendale—see?" The man merely prodded gently at the fly, causing it to start up again, buzzing insolently, up and around and around. "*Now* he might have a go, though."

The fly had come to rest on a much bulkier, richly carved but very robust-looking Chinese table, in a shaft of sunlight near the window.

"There!" growled the man, just as Bernard was uttering the same word—the man in anger, the ghost with satisfaction.

The paper came down with a terrific slap. The fly escaped at the very last instant. It headed for the interior door this time. Turner glared after it but gave up the chase and went back to his desk.

Joe, however, was still staring at the shaft of sunlight.

"Now *here's* where I can show you something," he said. "See all those particles of dust he's raised, swirling around in the sun? OK—so just watch me!"

Danny, Carlos and Karen grinned and nudged one another. They knew what was coming. Bernard and Samantha stared, mystified, as Joe slowly and deliberately placed a muscular arm and hand into the shaft of light.

He closed his eyes. His eyebrows came together, stiff with concentration. And then, slowly but surely, it happened.

The force that emanated from his forearm and wrist and the hand with its pointed finger began to attract the glittering particles. Their haphazard swirling began to slow down, to assume a definite direction, to cluster, to settle, until, there, hanging above the carved table, a ghostly outline took shape. *A wrist, a hand, a finger—the finger pointing accusingly straight at Turner!*

"Now *that* he would see!" said Carlos. "Those particles are still solid objects, small as they are. If only he'd look this way!"

"And get the fright of his life," said Karen.

But Turner was bent over his crossword.

Samantha nearly went berserk.

"Oh, *look!* Look, you fool! Look!"

She moved toward Turner, but Bernard grabbed her.

"It's no *use*, Sam! He can't hear you. Besides—Joe's finished now."

"Pow!" gasped Joe, withdrawing his arm. "It's

something you can't keep up for more than a few seconds at a time."

"Do you think *we* could do that?" said Samantha, shaking herself free from her brother's grasp.

"Sure!" said Joe. "Karen can. So can Carlos. Danny's improving. Sure. It just takes concentration. And lots of practice."

"You could do it with *any* light swirling objects," said Carlos. "Snowflakes, particles of moisture, like in a fog, even gnats."

"Gnats?"

"Sure!"

Samantha looked up at Bernard.

"There's always a swarm of gnats in the garden!" Then she frowned. "But of course these two louts never use it." She sighed. "Well—maybe it's just as well they don't. Otherwise they might find—"

Bernard interrupted her hurriedly.

"Let's show them the rest of the house. Upstairs, in the living quarters. Maybe there's something there that Joe could work on."

So they trooped out through the doorway in which the brother and sister had first appeared. Samantha was in the lead. She paused at the foot of the stairs to point along the corridor.

"There! That's where the garden is."

They saw a glass door with a fancy wrought iron screen, through which the light was pouring.

"It's closed, anyway," said Bernard, again sounding uneasy and in a hurry to change the subject. "Come on. They can see it from one of the upstairs windows."

But they never got any farther than halfway up those thickly carpeted stairs.

"Hey!" said Joe. "What's all this about?"

He was pointing at a picture hanging there.

It had been placed with its face to the wall.

"Oh, that!" said Samantha. "Need you ask? That's Mummy's portrait, and that pig downstairs is such a coward he always turns its face to the wall whenever Jackman's not here. He says it gives him the creeps—the creep!"

"He says her eyes always seem to follow him," said Bernard. "Jackman just laughs at him. Actually it's really very nice. A very good likeness. I'm sorry you won't be able to see it."

"Won't we?" said Joe, thoughtfully. "Won't we, though? Maybe this is where we *can* give him the fright of his life. Look at that plaster."

Probably with having been tugged at every time Turner reversed the heavy portrait and Jackman put it back, the hook had become loose. There was also the added leverage of the cord pulling outward instead of directly down, because of having to pass over the thick frame rather than behind it, as it normally did.

Whatever the cause, the plaster had begun to crumble around the nail.

Joe put his hand up, lightly passing his fingers a thousandth of an inch or less from the crumbling plaster.

"Gosh!" whispered Bernard, as one particle after another began to fall from the wall.

"Same principle as the dust," said Carlos.

"He did this with a bathroom medicine chest only a few weeks ago," said Danny, grinning. "You shoulda heard the crash *then!*"

"But it could take quite a long time," Karen warned them.

"Yes, but, oh boy, what a shock he'll get!" crowed Samantha. "I—"

She was interrupted by the ringing of the phone down below.

Joe stiffened.

"Hey!" he said, turning. "What time is it?"

Bernard shrugged. "It was getting on for twelve, the last time I looked."

"Never mind the silly old time, Joe," said Samantha. "Do get on with the plaster!"

But Joe wasn't listening. Not to her, not to any of them. He seemed to have ears only for the ringing, as he turned and went down the stairs three at a time.

The man was just lifting the phone when Joe and the others burst in.

"Anyone would think—" Samantha was saying.

"Yes?" said the man.

"—the call was for *him!* A *ghost!*"

Samantha sounded angry with Joe now.

"Who?" said the man.

Joe, and now Carlos and Danny and Karen, were standing as close as they could get, listening to the tinny but familiar voice at the other end.

"Miss Karen Hansen?" said Turner. "You must have the wrong number. There's no one of that name here."

Bernard and Samantha were now staring at Karen, pop-eyed.

Karen had started to blush.

"Don't you think we'd better explain, Joe?" she said as the man put the receiver down, oblivious of the shock *he'd* caused. "Part of it, anyway."

116

15
The Missing Link

Later, when the tense and terrible events of the next thirty-six hours were well behind them, Carlos would laugh about that moment.

"I mean the look on Joe's face! I mean there he'd been, lecturing *me—Careful, Carlos! Watch your mouth, Carlos!*—and now he'd almost given the secret away himself! All because he'd been too busy showing off his skills to remember to listen for the call and make sure that Samantha and Bernard didn't overhear it!"

By then, Joe could afford to laugh too, and he would aim a playful clout at Carlos's head that certainly didn't feel like the brush of a fly.

At the time, however, they all felt stunned for a few minutes: the American ghosts because their carefully arranged code had nearly betrayed them; and the British ghosts because they just didn't know what to think now.

"Somebody—somebody was asking for *you!*" said Samantha, shrinking away from Karen and going close to her brother.

"And it couldn't have been a ghost," said Bernard, looking from one to another of them, his eyes full of doubt and suspicion. "Ghosts can't pick up phones."

Joe was frowning, chewing at his lower lip.

"No . . ." he murmured. "That's true. They can't."

"So who was it, then?" said Samantha. "And—and—who are *you?*"

Joe took a deep breath.

"I can't tell you everything. But—please believe me—we are who we say we are. And we are your friends. We want to nail that guy—both those guys—as badly as you."

Turner was gazing out of the window at that point and glancing at his watch.

Bernard and Samantha still looked suspicious.

The others were watching Joe, wondering how much he would disclose.

"The call you just heard . . ." he began—then broke off for another chew at his lip.

"Yes?" said Bernard.

"Well . . . it's a sort of code. You weren't supposed to hear it. We didn't even know you'd be here, when it was devised."

"Devised with *who?*" insisted Bernard.

Joe ignored the question.

"We'd arranged for someone to call the first day. At twelve, your time. If anyone picked it up, the—the one at the other end would ask for one of us. If they asked for Mr. Gomez, it would mean nothing to report, everything OK this end. If they asked for Mr.

Armstrong, that would mean get back quick, Danny's mom and the kids are in immediate danger. And—and if they asked for Miss Karen Hansen, that would mean things are heating up but no real emergency yet."

Samantha was looking bewildered, Bernard still very suspicious.

"And Mr. Green?" he said, with a trace of sarcasm. "If they asked for Mr. Green—what then? Aren't you forgetting *that* name?"

He obviously felt that Joe was making all this up, patching together an elaborate excuse on the spur of the moment.

Joe wasn't shaken.

"No," he said. "Danny's name was out. We weren't sure whether Jackman had mentioned it to Turner or not when he'd been talking about Mrs. Green. If he had, the name might have alerted Turner. We didn't want to take any chances."

Bernard's expression was beginning to soften. But he still looked perplexed.

"But *who*, Joe? Who is this—this *someone?* To arrange all this, it would just *have* to be another ghost, wouldn't it?"

Then Samantha clapped her hands.

"Oh, Joe! Carlos! Don't tell me you've learned how we can use *phones?* I mean *do* tell me that! Oh, please!"

Her eagerness faded quickly as Joe shook his head.

"Well, no . . . that would be *too* difficult."

"You can say *that* again!" grunted Carlos.

"So—so it *was* a living person?" said Bernard.

"Of course. We . . . well . . ."

"So you've found a way to make contact?"

"Uh—sort of."

"Telepathy, I suppose?"

"Yeah—you could say that."

"Oh, but that's splendid! Marvelous! All we have to do to see that Jackman and Turner are punished is—"

Again Joe shook his head. Again Samantha's eagerness subsided.

"It isn't all that easy, honey," he said.

"You can say *that* again, too!" murmured Karen.

Then Bernard let Joe off the hook. Unwittingly. He took it that Joe meant the *telepathy* was not one hundred percent reliable—not the gathering of sufficient hard evidence to make sure the two rogues were brought to justice.

"I suppose it's a very hit-or-miss thing," he said. "Which method have you been—?"

His words were drowned by the clattering roar of a helicopter as it came flying low, directly over the buildings. Turner was peering up through the window, clucking with annoyance. The machine was so low it was even making the house vibrate.

That was when Joe was let off the hook once again. And not only Joe.

There came a loud thud and a crashing and bumping from the doorway leading to the stairs.

Turner swung round, but stayed fixed to the spot, horrified.

The ghosts were much quicker in their reflexes. Already they were on their way.

"It's Mummy's portrait!" cried Samantha. *"Look!"*

There was glee in her voice, but also a deep note of awe.

The picture had gone careening down from step to

step until now it lay facing them, propped askew against the bottom step, with the children's mother staring up at them. And she *was* a nice-looking woman, as Bernard had said. Her hair and eyes were dark like theirs, and her eyes were friendly and smiling.

But something had happened in the fall. The canvas seemed to have been caught on the edge of the banister or some other projection, and there was now a small rip in it. It was nothing very serious as far as damage to the painting was concerned—but it had occurred in the region of the mouth, giving the top lip a pucker that looked just like a horrible gloating sneer.

They heard a stifled scream behind them.

Turner had plucked up enough courage to investigate, but now that courage had left him again along with the scream. His face was whiter than ever. His Adam's apple was working rapidly. He was trembling all over.

Then, making a tremendous effort, he walked to the picture and, with eyes tight shut, picked it up and propped it against the wall, face inward.

"Get . . . get back where you belong!" he muttered. "Out of sight . . . you evil-looking—"

The rest of his mutter was drowned by Samantha's screams as she hurled herself at the man.

"Don't call my mother evil, you scum! Don't you dare! Don't you—"

"Sam! Take it easy! Stop it!"

"He—he called my mother—our mother—"

"I know, I know. But he's finished now. We have him now. We have them *both* now—Jackman, too."

His words had a steadying effect on his sister.

"You—you're not just saying that?"

Bernard shook his head. He was looking at Joe. His expression was very determined.

"I don't know just how strong your contact is," he said. "And I can see you don't want to go into details. But it's time that we *did*—Sam and I. It's time we took the chance and put our trust in you and told you *our* secret."

The Americans looked at one another, part puzzled, part surging with hope. Could this be *it?* Could this be what they had traveled all that distance for?

"Are you talking about—?" Joe began.

"Firm, solid evidence, yes," said Bernard. "I am going to show it to you." He glanced over toward the door of the showroom, where Turner had just, very shakily, returned. "But it's outside, and any minute now Turner will be leaving for lunch. So let's hold the explanations and make sure we slip out with him. It'll take him nearly a minute with the door half-open to fix the alarm system. He always fumbles it. But we'd still better be on our toes."

As it happened, there was no problem getting out, and once they were on the street Bernard began to explain.

"First," he said, "we'll go round the back, and I'll show you where the evidence is and how I came to know about it. Come on."

They followed in silence—too curious and excited to say anything—as he led the way, past the other stores in the block, then down a side street. It looked at first as if he were taking them away from the antique store altogether. But he led almost immediately down yet another side street, narrower than the first, and they realized that it ran along the backs of the stores they had just passed.

It was a cobbled cul-de-sac. Opposite the walls of the backyards belonging to the stores, there was a row of garages—most of them brightly painted—with living quarters above them. Originally, the garages had been stables, and the living accommodations had been for the use of coachmen and other servants. But now they were converted into small luxury apartments, with flowers in window boxes. Peering into the garages that were open, Danny spotted three Mercedes, a Rolls and a very racy-looking vintage sports Bentley, before they reached the dead-end.

"That's the back of our house," said Bernard, pointing to the L-shaped building with the L-shaped yard to match. "And this, through here, is part of our garden."

They stared through the thick black bars of the gate—the only viewpoint available in the high walls, topped with spikes.

It was quite a narrow strip of yard, with a path that led from the gate obliquely to the back door—the glass and wrought iron door they'd glimpsed from inside. In its present state, it hardly deserved being called a garden. Weeds sprouted from the cracks between the paving stones and choked the small flowerbeds at either side. They grew even more thickly in some of the ornate stone tubs, and coarse grass nearly obscured a sundial in the middle of what had once been a small square lawn. There was a large teak bench along the far edge of the square, its back facing the house, and next to it, on a pedestal about five feet high, a stone urn with fluted sides.

Weeds were sprouting from the urn, too.

"And that's where it is," said Bernard, softly. "In the urn."

"Oh? And what—?"

"Deep inside it," said Bernard, almost dreamily. "I made sure of that, thank goodness!"

"So—go on, Bernard. Tell them about it!" said Samantha.

Bernard nodded, brisk again.

"Yes. Well. It happened a few days before—before the car crash. Mummy, Sam and I had just returned from spending a couple of weeks by the sea. It seemed to do her good, getting away from Jackman. . . ."

But it hadn't lasted more than a few hours before the fights and the drinking flared up again, worse than ever. Jackman had been in a particularly nasty mood, and he seemed hell-bent on making them pay double for their short respite.

"Anyway, I used to spend a lot of time in the garden when it was fine, just to get out of the house. I didn't like to go far, in case Mummy really needed me, so I'd just sit there, pretending to read, but with one ear cocked all the time, listening for any signs of trouble."

"What about Sam?" asked Karen.

"Oh, I—I was a coward. Then. I—"

"You were *not*, Sam! There was nothing *you* could have done." Bernard turned to the others. "So I used to encourage her to go play with her friends as much as possible." He sighed. All the weight of his terrible responsibility seemed to be settling on his shoulders again. He gave them a shake. "Anyway, there I was, pretending to read. It was a sunny afternoon, and the

124

garden wasn't neglected then. Mummy saw to that, even right to the end. The grass was cut. There were flowers in all the beds and tubs. And in the urn there, there was a beautiful blue hanging plant, blue flowers spilling over like water."

Then he told them how his eye had picked up the glint of something in a clump of flowers at the side of the path.

"Someone over the garages must have opened a window, and the reflection of the sun swept over that part of the garden, otherwise I might never have spotted the thing myself. But the flash picked it up and caused the glint, and I went over to investigate. I thought it was probably a piece of broken glass."

"But it wasn't!" said Samantha, clapping her hands. "It was—"

"The missing link," said Bernard. "Yes."

"So what was it?" said Carlos, rather impatiently.

"Just that," said Bernard. "Or, to be even more precise, one half of a single cuff link. And a very expensive half too. Made of gold, with an emerald set in it. A fine-quality emerald, about a half-inch square. It alone must have cost thousands, so you can imagine what the full set was worth."

"But evidence of what?" said Joe. "And what made you hide it? Assuming that this *is* what's hidden in the urn."

"What it was evidence of, I didn't know at the time. What I did know, however, was that it didn't belong to either Jackman or Turner—otherwise we'd have heard about it, something that valuable. So I guessed it must have belonged to somebody else. A customer, perhaps, who'd been out in the garden to examine some small item in a strong natural light. It sometimes happened."

"But if—"

"If the link had been loose already, he might not have noticed it dropping at the time—especially with it landing in the flowers. And he might think he'd lost it somewhere else entirely."

"Couldn't you have asked Jackman or Turner if anyone had been in the yard recently?"

Bernard grinned at Karen.

"Are you kidding? And have them wanting to know why I asked? And getting suspicious? And finally getting it out of me? Jackman could be very persistent and nasty, you know, when he got suspicious. And I certainly wasn't going to hand the thing over to either of those two—the way you would to any decent honest person. No . . . I decided I'd say nothing and keep my eyes and ears open. Then if anyone came in inquiring about it or running a Lost ad, I'd deal with them direct."

"But why the urn?"

"Why not? I'd have to hide it somewhere until the real owner could be traced. And what better place could there have been than that? That was my thinking anyway. So I just reached up and pushed it into the soil—deep as I could—while I pretended to be plucking out some dead flowers. And there it still is."

They stared at the gray urn, with its dead brown stalks hanging from the rim and brighter green tufts of weeds sprouting at the top.

"I still don't know what you're getting at, though."

Bernard smiled at Joe.

"You will, in a few minutes. You will even see an

exact replica of that link, in full color. Just as if you had X-ray eyes and could see through that stone and soil. Come on."

"Yes, but—where?"

"To the nick!" Samantha laughed, dancing with excitement.

"The what?"

"The nick," said Bernard. "That's our word for police station. The cop shop, precinct house, or whatever you call it over there."

The police station turned out to be a big, gaunt, redbrick building a few blocks down the road from the antique store. A flight of wide stone steps led up to its entrance, but the six ghosts didn't go up those steps. There was a large glassed-in bulletin board at the bottom, to one side, and it was to this that Bernard and Samantha led the others.

"There!" said Samantha. "The Missing Link!"

They stared.

Among all the WANTED notices, it might have been overlooked by a casual browser. It had obviously been there for many months, and the sun had faded its colors somewhat. But the six ghosts had eyes for nothing else.

It was a close-up photograph of the link, exactly as Bernard had described it. The heading was in capitals.

HAVE *YOU* SEEN THIS CUFF LINK?

There was a small-print technical description of its material and dimensions underneath, followed, in larger type, by:

Police officers investigating the murder of Patrick James Conroy, whose body was found in a disused quarry near Datchworth, Hertfordshire, last September, would be grateful for any information regarding the article pictured above. Such information could help establish the location of the original attack—which might have been at a considerable distance from the place where the body was discovered. If you have found such an article, possibly without realizing its value, or know someone who has—or if anyone has offered such an article for sale—please contact the number below or any police station.

**All information will be treated
in strictest confidence.**

"And that's what you found?" said Joe, looking up at last and turning to Bernard. "In your garden?"

"That's what I found, right enough!"

"When did you first see this notice? I mean—"

"Oh, long after we'd been killed," said Samantha. "It wasn't till early December that we—well—woke up and found ourselves back here as ghosts."

"And even then," said Bernard, "the police had only just started advertising the clue. I suppose they'd been keeping it—uh—up their sleeves. Hoping to catch someone trying to sell it, maybe. Or making sure the murderers wouldn't make a thorough search at the scene of the crime and find it before they did."

"Jackman and Turner certainly made a thorough search when the news finally did come out!" said Samantha. "I remember the headlines in the paper Jackman was reading. Vital New Clue in Quarry

128

Murder, it said. Then: Have You Seen the Missing Link?"

Bernard nodded.

"That's when the news people started calling it The Missing Link Murder."

"But you should have seen the look on Jackman's face! And Turner's! They spent the rest of the day on their hands and knees, searching every inch of the showroom floors, the stairs, the living room up-stairs—then down again and into the garden!"

Bernard smiled at the memory—rather grimly.

"Yes. Even if we hadn't already heard them talking about it from time to time—Turner dithering, Jack-man very cool and confident—we could have recon-structed the crime just by watching where they con-centrated their search."

"What *did* happen?" Karen asked, wide-eyed.

"Yeah, and *when?*" added Danny, shuddering at the thought that right now one of those murderers might be sweet-talking his mother.

"It happened during the two weeks we were away at the seaside," said Bernard. "One evening. Late. Conroy was another crook—a swindler of some sort, like Jackman. He was wanting to set up some kind of a scam, involving an old lady with a houseful of an-tiques she didn't know the true value of. Fortunately for Jackman and Turner, Conroy was a bit of a loner. They'd never met him before, and he'd not told any-body he was going to see them. So there never was any link between him and them for the police to fol-low up on when the body was identified."

"Except *that* link, of course!" said Samantha, her eyes

already sparkling with triumph as she pointed to the notice.

"You figure they killed him in the house, then?" said Joe.

"We know they did," Bernard replied. "As I said, we've heard them talking about it often enough since. It seems Conroy suddenly turned nasty. He started to get the idea that they were out to cheat *him*—which was probably true."

"So then he started threatening Jackman and Turner with what he'd found out about them," said Samantha, who no longer seemed reluctant to utter the men's names. "Threatening to expose some of their dirty deals. He wasn't a big man, and Turner—who was much bolder in *those* days—started to get rough. Meaning to give Conroy a 'working over,' as he put it."

"But Conroy was stronger than he looked," said Bernard. "And Turner started to get the worst of it."

"And that's when Jackman came up behind Conroy and smashed him on the back of the head with a full bottle of gin." Samantha was looking fierce again. "As I said: not just an 'as-good-as-being-a-murderer.' A real one. Both of them."

The Ghost Squad members were looking very excited now. But Joe, cautious as ever, said:

"But supposing someone did find the link in the urn and reported it to the cops. It wouldn't necessarily *prove* these guys were the killers. Or even that the murder had taken place there."

"No," said Bernard, "but it would give the police reasonable grounds for thoroughly searching the house. And the car they carried the body away in."

130

"And then they'd be sure to find traces of blood on the carpets. We know there *were* some stains."

"They burned the car carpets, of course," said Bernard. "But the one upstairs is a valuable Turkestan. And they felt secure enough simply to give the spot a scrubbing and call that sufficient."

"Anyway," said Samantha, stepping lightly aside to make room for a couple of hefty young constables who were just leaving the building—and whose careers would have been made overnight if only they'd been able to hear the conversation they'd interrupted—"Anyway, once that kind of search is started, Turner will be *sure* to crack. Especially without Jackman here to boost him up or bully him into silence."

A slow grim smile was spreading across Joe's face. He was finally satisfied.

"We'll get right onto it," he said. "There's a six o'clock Concorde flight back to New York. Corrugation Factor or no Corrugation Factor, I think we should be on it."

Karen didn't hesitate.

"Suits me!"

"*And* me!" said Danny.

Carlos, the one who usually had the most to say when excited, was silent. His legs and hands had to express *his* joyful eagerness, as he danced from foot to foot in front of the notice, clicking his fingers.

Only his eyes remained steady, concentrating on the phone number it was his job to memorize.

16
The Very
Nasty Shock

And so, less than twenty-four hours after their arrival in London, the ghosts were on their way back.

Bernard and Samantha saw them off at the Hampstead tube station.

Bernard was still looking anxious, even though—without going into details—Joe had assured the brother and sister that their struggle to nail Jackman and Turner was nearly at an end.

"All you have to do is hang around and see what happens in the next couple of days. Of course, things can always go wrong at the last minute, but—well—you'll soon see. . . ."

Samantha believed him implicitly—just as if Joe had told them all about Buzz and Wacko. In fact, the change in her was quite dramatic. From being a half-wild creature almost animallike in her suspicion, she was now a normal happy kid again. The ghost of a kid, sure—but one that was looking forward to a major treat that was as sure as Christmas or her own birthday.

"And when it's all over," she said, "you must come again. Just for the fun of it, this time. We'll show you all the sights of London."

"I'd like that," said Karen.

"Not to see the queen, though!" said Samantha, laughing. "We heard what you were saying last night, up on the heath. And I'm afraid *that* trip just isn't on."

"Why?" said Karen, who'd since remembered something she'd once read. "Because the royal family goes to Scotland in the summertime? Or because of what Joe was saying about prying?"

"Neither," said Samantha. "Simply because you wouldn't have a chance. Bernard took me to Buckingham Palace once, when we first became ghosts. Hoping to cheer me up—right, Bernard?" But her brother was a little farther up the platform, deep in conversation with Joe, and he didn't hear her. "Anyway," she said, turning to the others, "it was no go. A complete waste of time."

"Why?" said Danny.

"Because even though we could slip past the living palace guards—even a few living intruders have managed *that*—we couldn't get past the ghost guards."

"Ghost *guards?*" said Carlos.

"Yes. The place is seething with them. Soldiers, policemen—people who died while still in the royal family's service. There were still some left over from Queen Victoria's time! That's why *they've* stayed

133

around as ghosts, I suppose. Their loyalty's fantastic! You wouldn't believe it."

Joe and Bernard were pretending to check the route to Heathrow on one of the wall maps. But their topic had nothing to do with lines and changing stations.

"I know you don't want to explain fully about your telepathy system," Bernard was saying. "And I'm not going to press for details. But gosh! I do hope it works this time."

"Look—don't worry. We—"

"Because if you can pull this off, Joe, you'll have done much more than make sure justice is done."

"I know. We'll have saved Danny's mother and brothers and sisters from—"

"Yes, yes! And something else. Something that could be even more important in the long run."

"Oh?"

"Yes. You'll have saved Samantha from turning into a full Malev!"

"Oh, I don't think . . ."

But even as he protested, Joe remembered the look on the little girl's face and her actions when her fury was in full force—and his words trailed off.

"And *therefore*," Bernard continued, "you'll have saved her from being doomed, doomed forever. And I mean at every level there might possibly be beyond this one."

Joe was grave now. He nodded.

"I hear what you're saying."

"Good!" Bernard's anxious frown lifted a little. "Because that's been *my* mission really, you know. Not revenge on Jackman, but trying to prevent *that* from

134

happening." He sighed. "And a right old mess I was making of it till you four came along."

"Hey!" said Joe, slapping him on the shoulder. "Cut it out! You were doing just fine! And—anyway . . . Uh-oh! Here comes the train."

There was one more parting scene before they finally left England. An unexpected one, this time.

They were threading their way through the crowds at the Heathrow international check-in area when a familiar voice called out.

"Going back already?"

It was Irma. She was looking very much more worried than when they'd last seen her. *Haggard* is rarely a word that can be applied to real ghosts, but in this case it came into all their minds as she hurried toward them.

"Yes—uh—we remembered some unfinished business."

She looked at Carlos so oddly when he said this, that Joe hurried to change the subject.

"You're looking sort of—uh—worried, Irma. Some problem?"

"The worst," she said. "I'm on my way back home myself. There isn't much *I* can do, but I feel I must be there. I— Remember what I was saying about trying to find out about terrorist plots? Especially any concerning my sister's flights? Well, finally I heard details of one this morning. . . ."

They listened, horrified, even forgetting their own business for a time, as she told them.

How, in two days' time, on the first London flight

of the day from Tel Aviv, a man would be boarding her sister's plane. How this man had been selected for a new kind of mission—a suicide mission—the aim of which was to blow up the aircraft as soon as it reached a certain altitude.

"And they've been very clever in their choice. He's one of them, of course, but he'll be posing as a French businessman. With perfectly genuine French papers. Because that is what he really is—now. He's been what's called a sleeper for several years—living and working as a Frenchman. He's even made the same trip a good many times already. But this time"—Irma shivered and closed her eyes for a moment—"this time he'll be carrying a bomb."

Carlos frowned and shook his head.

"But your country's airport security is the tightest in the world, Irma! They have the best equipment and the best-trained guards. He'll never make it. They search every bag and every suitcase, every package, pocket—hey, you name it!"

Irma was smiling sadly.

"Think I don't know about all that?" She shook her head, just twice. The smile went. "No. You see, this time the bomb will be *inside* the terrorist. In his stomach. How it works, I don't know. They got it from Bulgaria last week, and it's a completely new device. But he'll have swallowed it an hour or so before embarkation. The way they sometimes do for smuggling drugs or diamonds. In a sealed rubber bag. They— they're celebrating already."

"But he'll blow *himself* to pieces as well!" said Karen, incredulously.

Irma nodded.

"Like I said. It's a suicide mission. He probably can't wait to start out on it." Then, in a strange echo of Samantha's words, she said: "Their fanaticism is unbelievable."

Just then, the Concorde boarding call came over the loudspeakers.

"Look," said Joe, glancing at a nearby wall clock and patting Irma's arm, "don't worry. I mean that. Maybe there's something *we* can do to stop it."

"You?" Irma's eyes widened, almost angrily. Then they narrowed as she saw how serious the others were looking. "But how?"

"We've been experimenting," said Joe, giving Carlos a quick uneasy glance. "With—uh—telepathy. And there's a pretty good rapport between us and a living friend. OK?"

There was nothing angry in Irma's widened eyes now as she slowly nodded. Just astonishment—and growing hope.

"OK," said Joe. "We'll try and get through to him. Who would he have to call?"

"Oh, any of our airline offices or consulates. *They'll* take it seriously, all right. Especially if you use one of the code words that terrorists do use to prove that their warning calls are not hoaxes. When, of course, it suits the pigs to give warnings at all."

"Tell us one, quick!" said Carlos, beginning to dance.

"Well, one of the most recent ones is simply the statement: *There won't be a next time!*"

"There won't be a next time, huh?" murmured Joe. "OK. Well, try not to worry, Irma, because there isn't gonna be a *this* time! I mean, if that guy isn't stopped long before he's anywhere near the plane, it won't be our fault. . . . Now we've got to—uh—fly!"

And, leaving Irma staring after them thoughtfully, with that ray of hope still lingering in her eyes, the American ghosts went on their way.

The flight to New York was uneventful, smooth (apart from the Corrugation Factor, which not even Karen worried about this time) and fast.

It was so fast that they found themselves in New York earlier in the day than it had been in London when they took off.

But five o'clock is a busy time at Kennedy Airport, and it took them an hour to find a limousine that was going their way. Even then, the best they could do was clamber into the back of one that was heading for a town about twenty miles from their own. Fortunately, however, it was on the same rail line, and from there they were able to get a train to their destination without much waiting around.

Thus, toward sundown, they rolled into their hometown station and got off with a few late commuters. On this last leg of the journey—which seemed unbearably slow—they'd been wondering if they'd be able to find Buzz and Wacko before it was too late to do anything else that day.

As they started to make their way between the cars still parked on the railroad station lot, they had a pleasant surprise.

"Hey!" cried Danny. "There's Buzz now! Over by the guardrail at the . . ."

His voice trailed off.

For that's when they all had a very nasty shock.

"But—but—" Karen looked even more horrified than when she'd first encountered the Corrugation Factor. "But who—*what*—who or *what* is he *talking* to?"

They stood there—all four of them—frozen.

They were staring at Buzz and Wacko's mysterious helper.

17
The Elemental

Buzz had been having a frustrating day.

Getting up in time to make the seven o'clock call to London hadn't created any problem, heavy sleeper though he normally was. Last night had been mostly spent tossing and turning, worrying about whether they'd been wise to enlist an unknown ghost as a helper, and he'd been wide awake long before seven.

Nor had Buzz worried much about putting in an international call.

"The Phillips house is a democratic house," his father had long since declared. "Every member can phone anyone, anywhere, without asking permission. So long as each person pays for his or her own calls at the end of the month."

Even the expense hadn't worried Buzz unduly. A short call to London would cost less than five dollars, and Wacko had promised to go halves.

No; it was the call itself that had set the uneasy tone for Buzz's day. Because, OK—someone had replied at the antique store, and Buzz had been able to get his code message across. But to whom? How was he to know that the ghosts had been listening in? What if they hadn't been able to get into the store in time? Or into the room where the phone was?

If only they'd been able to shout over the man's shoulder: "Message received, Buzz!"

Maybe they did, at that. It would have been just like Carlos.

But if Buzz couldn't hear them when they were actually present, how could he expect to hear them over the phone?

Frustrating was the word.

And then there was the 9 A.M. meeting with the helper.

Oh, he'd turned up all right. On the dot. He seemed very efficient in carrying out simple orders. But beyond that, he seemed so *dumb*.

It had taken them nearly half an hour to get to know that:

(1) there had as yet been no firm proposal of marriage;

(2) Jackman had gone back to his hotel, later the previous night; and

(3) the helper had followed him there.

Beyond that: zilch.

As far as Buzz and Wacko had been able to gather, the helper had simply sat in Jackman's room, or stood there like some dumb sentry, watching the sleeping man. He hadn't even been able to say if Jackman had made or taken any calls. He didn't seem to understand what they were asking him. The words *call*, *phone*, and *telephone* just drew a blank silence. Maybe he was a foreigner who knew very little of the language.

So they'd dismissed him, ordering him to continue his surveillance and report again at eight-thirty in the evening. To which he'd replied with a very smart touch to each boy's right ear—crisp and alert once again.

In fact, that's all it turned out to be: a surface crispness. After all, during the rest of the day, Buzz and Wacko had found out as much as he did, for all his extra advantages.

For instance, they'd spotted Jackman's station wagon outside the public library, shortly after ten—and they weren't surprised to see him at a table in the local history corner of the reference room, poring over maps and old books.

"Looks like he's still researching the treasure," whispered Wacko, as they stayed over by the door, not wishing to let Jackman know they'd spotted him.

And Jackman had still been there at the end of the morning.

Mrs. Green, meanwhile, had been resting in bed—probably nursing a hangover. But she was up in time to join Jackman and the kids for another picnic lunch at Sentinel Pond that afternoon. This time Jackman had gone easier on the kids, leaving them to play by the pond while he went and prodded among trees just beyond the blighted bowl.

After that, he'd taken them all for another treat, this time to a mansion that was open to the public. It had a local history museum, which the kids might have found boring, if there hadn't also been a small animals zoo on the same property, with pony rides.

All this the boys had found out for themselves when the family returned with Jackman shortly after six, and they'd questioned Mike while Jackman was indoors. And at eight-thirty, when Buzz had come alone for the appointed debriefing session with the helper, the latter had only been able to confirm all this, without adding a single scrap of new information.

"Was Jackman researching *there*, too? At the museum place?"

There was no response.

"Do you understand what I'm saying?"

Left ear.

"Was Jackman—uh—studying old books and maps there?"

Right ear.

"Terrific," said Buzz, sourly. "So what is your opinion? Does he still believe he's close to finding some treasure?"

Nearly a minute went by before Buzz felt a touch on his right ear. He translated it as being a doubtful "Mm—yes—well—maybe."

"OK. So how about Mrs. Green, then? Is she any closer to deciding to marry Jackman?"

No answer.

"Well, does she show any *sign* of being any nearer?"

No answer.

Buzz groaned. He felt snappish. He was tired. He was so tired he even felt a sneaking resentment that Wacko had had to go out to dinner with his family that evening, to celebrate his mother's birthday. Buzz stamped on that resentment as soon as he recognized it—but it still left him with a strong feeling that Karen had been right. This *was* getting too complicated for yes/no questions.

He sighed and switched to simple queries about the helper himself.

"You told us this morning you were thirty-two years old. Right?"

The brush on the right ear came swiftly, even a trifle impatiently. After all, it had taken eleven yes/no questions to elicit that much.

"Yes, well, I wanted to ask you—how long have you been a ghost? Less than a year?"

Left ear.

"More than a year?"

Right ear.

"More than two years?"

Right ear.

The helper seemed very sure of himself now. Thinking that this dumb chitchat questioning, so easily answered, might sharpen the ghost's reflexes, Buzz kept on. And he'd just reached the more-than-ten-years mark and was beginning to get really curious, when the responses suddenly ceased.

This, had he but known it, was the point at which Joe and the others took over. And it was just as well, because otherwise he'd have had a long session ahead of him.

The helper in fact had been a ghost for more than *two hundred* years!

This much had been obvious to Joe and the others right at the start.

The uniform that Buzz's companion was wearing proclaimed it at once. It was that of a British soldier

144

at the time of the Revolution: red coat, cocked hat, white leggings, with crossed shoulder straps for the side pouches. There was even a musket, complete with bayonet, slung over his left shoulder.

Everything was in good condition—up to a point. The musket looked as if it had just been lovingly oiled. The walnut stock gleamed. The bayonet shone. The coat was a rich scarlet, and the white straps were spotless.

But the point beyond which the stooping figure, listening intently to Buzz, stopped being historically colorful and became a matter for horror, concerned its outlines.

There were great chunks missing: in the thighs, especially the left one, and the torso, where it seemed that the whole of the right lung and rib cage had been torn away—or, rather, *bitten* away—by some monster with huge jaws. And what made the sight even more horrifying was that these weren't simply wounds, however ghastly. There were no frayed and ragged edges of cloth and flesh, no splintered bones, no blood stains. Like all ghosts everywhere and in all ages, the man's clothes and body didn't bear the marks of what had actually killed him.

No. The edges were smooth. They reminded Carlos of certain rocks worn into curious shapes by the action of winds or waves over a prolonged period. They reminded Karen, on the other hand, of the disfiguration of a plastic salad server that had fallen onto the heating element of the dishwasher. There was the same almost glossy finish of the edges of those deep bites— as if the man's body too had been warped by an intense heat.

But Carlos's impression came closer to the truth.

These were indeed the erosions of time. Two centuries of time. On a ghost body.

"Is this—is it one of the Mad Ones?" gasped Danny, who'd heard of such beings but never seen anything like this before.

Joe nodded grimly.

"Some ghosts call them that, yes. Others call them Elementals."

Joe preferred the latter term. For these weren't just crazy. They were not even Malevs. No. These were the fanatics of the ghost world. And their fanaticism was so deep that it kept them going for years and years, even centuries, like this one. Burning with some passionate devotion to a single cause. Or with a single-minded lust for revenge—what they regarded as *righteous* revenge.

The man who was prepared to blow himself up with the airliner might well become one. *He* wouldn't regard his act as suicide. Neither would his comrades. Self-sacrifice in a just cause, yes. And there were obviously a few such hanging around the palace in London, judging from Samantha's description. In fact, now that Joe came to think of it, Samantha herself had been well on the way to becoming one. Not a Malev. An Elemental. Which was much more terrible. Even Malevs were scared of Elementals. They were the nearest that ghosts got to seeing ghosts of ghosts—and the regular ghosts felt something of the same terror that a living person would at seeing a regular ghost.

The Railroad Street area right now proved that. Usually, at most times of the day or night there would be a few ghosts around, mingling with the living, busy on their own affairs.

Not now, though.

Except for themselves and the redcoat, there wasn't a single ghost to be seen. All the rest had fled, like small birds when a hawk appears. Except in this case there wouldn't be any watching from their hiding places. Ghosts have superstitions just like the living, and one of the strongest of these is that when an Elemental comes walking abroad from his remote lair, it is to recruit or even capture any ghost that catches his eyes. One look would be enough too, according to some. One direct glance from the eye of an Elemental, and you disappeared from other ghosts forever— to be transported instantly to Hell.

But this one was communicating with Buzz.

"I don't know about you guys," murmured Joe, "but we can't just walk away."

For a full minute, no one moved or spoke.

Then, in a shaky voice, Danny said, "You bet we can't. . . ."

"We—we must be very careful, though," Karen whispered.

Suddenly Carlos exploded.

"Superstitious rubbish!" he hissed. He'd been fighting his fear, trying to stamp the unhealthy life out of it, and for the moment he'd succeeded. "I once ran a test. On the Mad Lady of Gallows Hill. She looked at me, and she laughed in a horrible way, and she screamed, but all she did was say, 'Go! Get gone!' Just like she was a living lady who'd caught me trespassing in her orchard. And *I* didn't get carried away or disappear."

The ghost he talked about was well known to them by reputation—the town's most notorious Elemental, and the only one most of the local ghosts knew about. Very few would have dared to do what Carlos had done. In fact, this was the first the other three had heard of it. So much in the spirit of scientific curiosity had Carlos conducted the test, it had never occurred to him to brag about it.

His report did a lot to boost Karen's courage. Joe himself seemed reassured.

"Come on! Let's see what it's all about."

But as they drew nearer, walking warily, some of their courage began to fade. Even Carlos's.

And when Joe said softly, "Sir?" and the soldier swung around, Karen had to stifle a scream and the others gasped.

If the sight of the holes from a distance and with the Elemental's back turned had been gruesome, what they saw now was like the worst kind of nightmare.

That *face!* The nose—

But the nose was missing.

In its place was a dark, dark hole.

Again, there were no ragged edges, no signs of a wound. Just an erosion—filled with a strange gray blankness that none of the Ghost Squad was able to penetrate or even properly focus on. They certainly couldn't see into it or through it, as with regular cavities or holes in weathered stone. And, as their eyes flinched away, they saw it was the same with the larger gaps further down the body. Just a misty dimness that

148

suggested the mouths of deep shadowed pits or fissures.

"Aye?"

The voice was thin, distant—but mild enough.

They raised their eyes. And to avoid that pit where his nose had once been, they were forced to look the soldier straight in the eyes or watch his mouth.

They were not frightening, anyway.

His eyes were a clear blue gray, and his gaze was steady and unblinking. The mouth was broad and unsmiling, but not ill-tempered. When he spoke, he revealed strong white teeth; when he was silent, the lips closed firmly but without being compressed into a thin line.

"We—we saw you talking to this person," said Joe, nodding toward Buzz, who was sitting on the guardrail. "He—"

"Stay! Or . . . consequences!"

Two things caused Karen to scream out loud and the others to tremble.

One: the eeriness of the voice, like wind in a distant stand of trees, with breaks of complete silence.

And Two: the lightning speed with which the musket seemed to leap from the man's shoulder and be presented at Joe, with the point of the bayonet less than an inch from his throat.

The contrast of the two—the ancient feebleness and the present vigor—was devastating.

Joe gulped. He had only intended to give Buzz a friendly warning touch on the top lip: the regular signal to show their living colleagues that they were back again after an absence.

But the soldier seemed to have taken it as some kind of threatening act.

The point of the bayonet gleamed under the reddening sky.

Joe repressed another shudder.

That musket, he knew, could never be fired to kill another ghost, unless perhaps the muzzle were in direct contact with the victim. The ball would disappear as soon as it left the muzzle, just as Samantha's spittle had when leaving her lips. The weapon was simply a part of what the soldier considered his essential dress, the one he felt best in or most comfortable in when alive.

But the bayonet was a different proposition, as far as being lethal to another ghost was concerned. So long as the soldier held onto that weapon, the wickedly winking blade could stab or slice another ghost just as effectively as it had no doubt acted on living men two centuries ago.

"Peace!" Joe managed to whisper. "We don't mean any harm. He—he's a friend of ours."

The bayonet point was withdrawn. By no more than another inch. Again the frail reedy voice issued from the strong vigorous mouth.

"This lad . . . a friend? Yours? . . . Can . . . furnish his name?"

"Buzz. Buzz Phillips."

The bayonet went back another inch. Then held steady.

"True enough. But . . . name of his friend, the black . . ."

"Wacko. Wacko Williams."

This time the bayonet was withdrawn several inches.

150

"Aye. True enough . . . droll names . . . but true enough."

The eyes narrowed slightly. And hardened. Even the voice seemed to become firmer.

"And their enemy? . . . his name? . . . Come on, come on, lad! . . . Their chiefest enemy?"

"Uh—Jackman?"

It was like a password—or the culmination of a series of passwords. The musket and bayonet were suddenly withdrawn altogether. With the same suddenness as it had been presented, the weapon was slipped back over the redcoat's shoulder.

"Aye!" The sigh was very treelike this time. A long gust of chill wind rattling the dying autumn leaves. " 'Tis so."

"Rick Jackman," said Joe, emboldened to follow up. "Richard. He's our enemy too."

"Rick . . ." The lips had a bitter twist now. "Richard . . . Alas! Aye . . . If t'were only *Seth*." The soldier lifted his eyes to the red and purple sky. "If only it had pleased the Almighty . . . to grant me Seth. *My* Jackman. *Seth* Jackman . . . *Seth Jackman* . . ."

During this encounter, Buzz had been asking in a low voice if anyone was still there. No one had answered. This confrontation between ghosts was too important. Certain matters had to be cleared up on both sides. So Buzz had finally shrugged and muttered, "Summer help! They're all alike. I guess I'll just have to sit it out and keep watch on my own."

"This Seth Jackman," said Joe. "Is he—was he—any relation?"

"Aye, lad, aye!" The voice was stronger again, more

human, so much so that they could hear the British north-country accent. "The dead spit an' fetch of this 'un. . . . I nearly thought I had him at last."

"And was *he*—?"

"The biggest scoundrel an' scamp as ever walked the face of this earth. . . . Livin' or dead."

Then the redcoat told them of the man he so sinisterly referred to as *his* Jackman, and how they had come to meet each other, and what had happened to make that man the soldier's enemy not just for life but for all eternity.

"First, you must know my name is Tom Bowes," he began. "Corporal Tom Bowes . . . and I came here in the service of my king and country . . . year of our Lord seventeen hundred and . . ."

It was a mild enough beginning, with the voice well under control, like a light steady breeze. But before the story was ended, the four listeners caught echoes, and more than echoes, of gusts and gales and storms, and at least one hurricane, with its own central eye of deadly stillness and silence, before it raged on again with greater fury than ever to the devastating, desolating end.

18
The Redcoat's Story

Corporal Tom Bowes had been one of a body of men picked to form a kind of special operations unit. This had been the brainchild of Major John André, aide to the British commander in chief, General Sir Henry Clinton.

The aim: to establish a British stronghold in the Connecticut hills deep inside American-held territory, from which to harass the enemy and, if successful, to be the pivot of a chain of similar strongholds.

The site: the plateau beyond Sentinel Pass, thickly wooded and with steep sides, capable of being defended by a small number of crack troops against an army, if necessary.

The men: seasoned regular fighters from the Grenadiers and various foot regiments, with a number of

Mohawk scouts, all under the command of Major "Mad Harry" Halliday.

When the corporal mentioned that name, both Carlos and Danny caught their breath and looked at each other, remembering the box of papers they'd seen in Jackman's hotel room.

"Dost' know him, lad?" asked the redcoat, whose eyes and ears seemed to miss nothing.

He was looking at Danny.

"Uh—no—I mean yes. Yes, sir. Only I thought it was *Colonel* Halliday."

". . . seen the box then?" said the corporal, not without a glimmer of respect.

"Yes, sir."

The redcoat nodded.

" 'Tis the same. . . . At the time, early in 'eighty, he was Major. . . . And a brave rogue he was!" he continued. "A rogue of a man, but the bravest of the brave . . . as a soldier and leader. . . ."

Halliday had been given only a couple of months to lick his new unit into shape. And then, with the first thaws of late February, they had started—in small groups of ten or a dozen men, each group from a different point—on their fifty or sixty miles' trek to Sentinel Mountain.

"Marching only at nights . . . resting by day . . . in backwoods-men's clothing . . . that we might be mistaken merely for marauding bands of ruffians should we be seen. . . . But . . . never were. The training had been so excellent . . . the scouts so watchful."

The biggest problem apparently, apart from late snowfalls and subzero temperatures, had been the baggage.

154

"We had to carry our equipment, our tools, our basic stores, as well as . . . folded regimentals, extra ammunition . . . and the gold . . . so necessary . . . every step of the way."

"Gold, sir?" whispered Carlos.

The corporal's eyes twinkled briefly.

"Aye, lad! The British sovereigns. A prince's ransom. And right heavy they weighed . . . I *know*. I was one of those entrusted with them."

The money was essential to the plan. Once installed in their stronghold, the British would never have been able to remain there long—impregnable though it was—without the help of local inhabitants.

"For food, yes . . . but mainly ammunition. Ammunition and information. To be . . . paid for . . . in British gold."

"You're talking about a traitor, huh?" said Joe, grimly.

"Aye, lad! I am. A traitor and a spy. . . . And I too despise the sort. All soldiers do . . . all true soldiers . . . whether the traitors be helping them or no."

Major André, in charge of British Intelligence, had long since had a candidate in mind. In the scattered backwoods communities of the area, there was a certain fairly prosperous farmer who was looked on by his neighbors as an honest man and an outspoken critic of the British.

"Honest, he could never ha' been. A hater of the British . . . perhaps. But above all else, above family and neighbors and the American cause—above God Himself—that man loved money. . . . His name . . . Seth Jackman."

The listeners murmured. They were beginning to

see. They had no difficulty whatsoever in substituting *their* Jackman for this one.

"He had been well prepared by André. . . . He knew what was required . . . and he did it. . . . If Sir Henry's plan had ever succeeded, and we had by its means defeated Washington's army . . . even capturing or killing the general himself on his visit to Hartford later in the year . . . Seth Jackman would have been chiefest to thank. . . ." The eyes twinkled briefly again, no doubt noticing the scowls in front of him. "Or, in course, to *blame*."

Then he shrugged.

"But who is a traitor to one, can be a traitor to t'other. Jackman began to . . . difficulties. It soon became known by the hill folk . . . as months went by . . . that we were there . . . and not only there, but there in strength . . . and not only in strength, but receiving aid. Tongues began to wag. . . . Who, they asked among themselves, could it be? . . . Th'art looking puzzled, lad."

Carlos nodded.

"Yes. I mean how did *you* know, sir, up there, what they were saying in the villages around you?"

The redcoat's smile was wide—but ghastly.

They guessed that Carlos had touched some very tender nerve.

"There . . . there were connections . . . with a few . . . not based on gold . . . or hate . . . or matters military. There were meetings . . . secret meetings . . . for transactions . . . private . . . one to one other."

Joe, Carlos and Danny looked puzzled. Only Karen

seemed to have any idea what the soldier was talking about. It couldn't have been the reflection from the sky that reddened her cheeks now.

"Girls?" she whispered.

The corporal nodded sadly.

"Yes, my bonny young lass. In particular *a* girl. Not unlike yourself . . . but more properly clad. Her name was Sue. She lived with her father, in a cabin, near the pass. We met one day in early spring. I was patrolling the woods; she . . . she was gathering ferns . . . fiddleheads, she called them. And that is what we talked about. Not wars . . . not supplies . . . not the disposition of troops or sentries . . . fiddleheads."

The last words came out as the softest of whispers.

Again the smile—forced, ghastly—stretching the lips over the strong teeth so tight it was impossible for them to tremble.

"I said, 'Nay, lass, th'art never going to *eat* those things?' And she . . . she said, 'Yes, for sure, when properly cooked they are delicious.' And the next day . . . in the same place . . . she brought some with her . . . properly cooked . . . and they were delicious."

"They are," whispered Karen. "I've tried them."

The soldier nodded.

"So, yes . . . we fell in love. We talked of nothing else but that . . . and fiddleheads . . . and how we would be married . . . just as soon . . ."

He took a deep breath and glared at them.

"*She* was not a spy! Nor a traitor. Always . . . everywhere . . . your *own* troops, later, much later.

157

Did *they* not fall in love and marry and bring home as wives the daughters and sisters of the men they'd been fighting? . . . From Prussia, and Saxony, and the Orient? I have seen them in this town. . . . 'Tis only natural."

"You bet!" said Karen, giving the others a glare of her own. "My grandmother was a war bride. From Frankfurt, Germany!"

Nobody was arguing.

"So what happened to Jackman, sir?" said Danny. "Did they catch him?"

The soldier had hung his head. The face was obscured by the hat. The hat shook.

"No," he murmured. "They did not. He . . . he used his influence . . . and three . . . just *three* . . . of his traitor's sovereigns . . . to make it appear that . . . traitor was someone else. . . . So he secreted them . . . the three doubly traitorous sovereigns . . . while Sue and her father were seeking a strayed hog. . . . He secreted them in the chest . . . the chest she was using . . . for wedding clothes."

Suddenly his head jerked up, his heels snapped together, and, standing at attention, he cried as loud as his reedy voice would let him:

"Oyez! Oyez! Be it known that Susan Bierce, daughter of Adam Bierce and the late Emily Bierce, hath been consorting with an enemy soldier and hath received British gold for her services as spy and comforter and provisioner of the garrison beyond the pass!"

Then he slumped again and continued, in gasps:

"In such . . . words . . . Jackman denounced her . . . and they . . . hanged her . . . in sight of the British camp . . . until . . . she . . . dead."

158

There was a long pause. The life of the town went on around them. Buzz suddenly got up and crossed the road. He'd spotted Mike. But none of the listeners paid any attention.

The soldier drew himself together.

" 'Twas all one to me, after that. Two weeks later . . . regiment of French dragoons was summoned to the area. We fought; we lost. I myself was killed. . . . Jackman had been able to supply the French with too many details about our strength . . . our weak points. There must ha' been many and many a French louis added to his hoard of sovereigns."

The word *hoard* alerted Carlos.

"What about Major Halliday, sir?"

A faint smile came to the soldier's lips.

"Ah, *that* rogue! He fought like a lion, like ten lions. He fell wounded . . . was taken prisoner . . . treated as a guest of honor by the French. . . . Later he was sent home . . . to continue in the army and rise . . . rank of colonel."

"But why do you call him a rogue?" Joe asked.

The eyes above the void twinkled again.

"Why? Because he was. He, remember, was Jackman's paymaster. . . . He had been told by Major André to pay . . . only what was necessary . . . for what he received. But rogue as he was . . . and they too are in every army, everywhere . . . Halliday gave Jackman *double* . . . on the understanding . . . when the British had reconquered the colonies . . . Jackman would share the extra with him."

But, of course, history hadn't worked out that way, and Jackman got to keep the lot.

"Ah, if only Mad Harry hadn't been killed . . . a

duel back in England four years later! There would have been such a reckoning as never was! He had been planning to return to America . . . even had a notion of where Jackman kept his hoard. . . . But now . . . 'tis left to me. And I . . . I have a score to settle . . . far greater than a tub of paltry coins."

"Do you—do you think Seth Jackman will ever come back, sir?"

The grin again.

"Yesterday, when I saw *your* Jackman up by the pass, I thought he had. . . . Then I saw he was in the flesh and untouchable by me and so could not be mine. . . . I followed him and them . . . the goodwife and her children . . . and accompanied them in the horseless carriage, to be quite sure. Like, *very* like, this one is—but not mine." He shrugged. "However, 'twas because of that . . . I made the acquaintance of your friends."

He glanced across the street.

Buzz was just finishing talking to Mike. He still looked fed up.

Then the soldier turned to Joe and said, in crisp military tones:

"Your Jackman is yours. Be wary of him for your friends' sake. . . . He is every whit as wicked. . . . But what is yours is yours. . . . I shall now return and await *mine*. . . . He will surely be back . . . one day." He sighed, then, bowing slightly to Karen and giving the others a smart salute, said: "So I'll bid ye all a good night and . . . fair going to ye!"

And, whistling softly, he marched off down the street.

160

They watched him go, each with his or her own thoughts.

Karen had recognized the tune he was whistling and was thinking about that. She'd learned to play it on the fife, for a school pageant play about the British surrender at Yorktown. It was called "The World Turned Upside Down," and she was thinking, Oh, boy!

Carlos's thoughts were more in the present. As he watched the receding figure—eroded but erect—its red coat still retaining the glow of the fading daylight—Carlos had a vision of all the ghosts between Railroad Street and Sentinel Pass shrinking away before the Elemental corporal.

"Like in the old Western movies when the terrible hired gun walks through town," he mused. "Only this would be the Fastest *Musket* in the *East*."

Then he gulped when he realized that it was no matter for joking. Superstition or not, they had only just emerged unscathed from a situation of maximum peril.

The thoughts of Joe and Danny were more practical.

"Shouldn't we let Buzz know we're here?" asked Danny.

"You took the words right out of my mouth," said Joe.

"Hey!" cried Buzz, when he felt a touch on his upper lip. "Danny?

Right ear.

"All of you?"

Right ear.

"But I didn't give you the red alert call this morning!"

Left ear.

"I mean, you *heard* my call?"

Right ear.

Buzz's eyes widened.

"So—so *you* have something? About Jackman? Already?"

Three right ears.

"What? I mean, is it—? Oh, gosh! We need Wacko's word processor for this, don't we?"

Right ear.

"But he's gone out for the evening. I— Can it keep until tomorrow morning?"

There was a pause. They were looking at one another. There was no code for "I guess it'll *have* to!"

So Joe just touched him on the right ear.

"OK! Fine! Look. I'll get in touch with Wacko first thing tomorrow morning and fix a meeting at his place. How about eight-thirty?"

Right ear.

"Great! But—oh, boy!—I wish you could tell me *something*. Like—is it—do we have enough to stop Jackman?"

Then Danny gave him *four* on the right ear, which clearly meant, "Yes! In spades!"—and with that, Buzz had to be content for the whole of another restless night.

19
Showdown
at Sentinel Pass

The meeting of the Ghost Squad the following morning was the busiest they'd ever had. Right from the first flicker of the word processor's screen, Joe insisted on absolute priority for their report on the London trip—focusing on what they had discovered at both Heathrow and Hampstead. Even then, it took them over an hour to get across to Buzz and Wacko all the important details.

First Joe—through Carlos and the word processor—told the boys about Irma and her story, while Buzz noted the details of the bomb plot scheduled for the next day: the description of the phony Frenchman, the type of bomb (not forgetting its possible country of origin), the flight targeted and the code message to ensure that his call would be given serious attention.

Then the two living members learned about Bernard and Samantha and their story. They were told about Conroy's murder, with very precise details of the missing link, its hiding place, the exact location of the urn, and the fact that the bottle used as the murder weapon was the square-sided kind.

"That could be very useful as backup information," Carlos had insisted. "The medical examiner's report will probably have indicated just that kind of weapon."

The ghosts also gave prominence to what the brother and sister had told them about the car rugs' being burned and, especially, the traces of blood probably still adhering to the Turkestan rug upstairs.

Buzz made notes of all these points too, together with the phone number that Carlos had memorized from the police notice.

"Right," he said, looking up from his notebook after reading back to them both sets of details. "Well, with the bomb business, I'll call the consulate in New York. It's too important to be fooling around with airline offices." He looked at his watch. "And since it's already mid-afternoon in London, I'll get onto the Conroy murder business and call *that* number as well."

"You think you can manage to make the calls in private OK?" said Wacko.

"No problem," said Buzz. He grinned. "Ours is a democratic household, remember." Then his grin wobbled slightly. "It's gonna cost us at the end of the month, though." He shrugged. "But who cares about *that* with emergencies like these on our hands?"

"*Correct!*" came the answer on the screen. "*We have had an idea for raising some funds for Ghost Squad expenses. But we'll discuss that later.*"

"Good!" said Buzz. "Hey—but before I go, how about telling us who we hired as summer help. My guess is it was a foreigner—right?"

There was a pause. Then the message came back:

"You could say that. But we'll discuss that later, too. In the meantime, a word of warning. Don't you ever, either of you—repeat, ever—do anything like that again. OK?"

The two boys looked at each other guiltily.

"No, we—uh—"

"But—"

"Later! Right now, Buzz, go. Make the calls. Then come straight back and report. We'll be waiting for you. And— hold it! One more thing: Do not—repeat, not—tell them at the other end who is calling. The details should speak for themselves."

Buzz grinned again as he went to the door.

"Think I'm stupid or something?"

And he was already on his way when Carlos got an answer across to that one.

"After last night, buddy, we're beginning to wonder!"

The ghosts spent the next fifteen minutes or so finding out from Wacko just what he and Buzz had been doing in their absence—besides jeopardizing the whole operation by parleying with unknown ghosts.

So Wacko told them about the two picnics and the phony treasure hunt and what Mike and Jilly had been able to tell them. Also of Jackman's researches in the library and later at the museum.

"But that was all, I guess," he ended. "I mean, we got nothing like the stuff you guys turned up."

Carlos took pity on him and said, through the screen:

"You did OK. And there were four of us, don't forget. With better access behind the scenes."

But the main topic between the other ghosts just then was the mention of the search for the old root cellar so close to Sentinel Pass.

"It looks like Jackman might have stumbled onto something big in that box of papers," said Joe.

"You mean the *other* Jackman's hoard?" said Karen.

"Yeah." Then Joe shrugged. "Anyway, it also looks like his treasure hunt's gonna be cut short very soon now."

"If there *is* any treasure still up there," said Danny, more interested in removing the danger to his family.

The ghosts didn't say anything to Wacko about Tom Bowes and his story. That would have to keep until Buzz could hear about it too. And even when Buzz returned, twenty minutes later, there were still some other more urgent matters to be dealt with first.

"How did the calls go?" Wacko asked.

"No problem. The consulate kept me on hold a few minutes while they dug out someone with a high enough rank. But the London police didn't mess around at all."

"I hope they took it seriously," said Wacko.

"Oh, they did that, all right! You shoulda heard their voices—both places—when I started giving details. . . . You guys still around?"

"Affirmative!" Carlos flashed back. *"We're listening. Go right ahead."*

"So what'll happen next, I wonder?" said Wacko, frowning. "About Jackman, I mean."

"Scotland Yard will search the urn, find the link,

pick up on the bloodstains and send someone across to collar Jackman," said Buzz. "What d'you *expect* them to do? Send him a medal?"

"It isn't that easy," said Wacko. "There'll have to be extradition proceedings. It could take several days."

That pulled up more than Buzz. The ghosts were looking troubled now. Wacko's father was a lawyer, and, concerning matters legal as well as scientific, Wacko generally knew what he was talking about.

"So Jackman could still give us the slip!" gasped Danny.

Carlos translated it to the screen, verbatim.

Wacko read it and nodded.

"If he gets forewarned—yes."

"Yes, but who—?" Buzz began.

"His buddy. This Turner guy. Who else?"

"But Turner won't have the *chance!* He'll be under arrest, as soon as they find that link."

"Sure," said Wacko, patiently. "But before they find the link, they'll have to search the premises. And for that, they'll need his permission."

The ghosts had been listening to this exchange with taut expressions, turning from one to the other of the boys as if it had been an exciting game of tennis.

Those expressions lightened a little when Buzz said:

"Unless they get a search warrant. *Then* they won't need Turner's permission."

Wacko shook his head—and five faces fell.

"In a case like this, they'll probably just ask first. They don't know if it might be a hoax. If he refuses, of course, they'll be more suspicious. In that case, they'll return with a warrant in a few hours. *Possibly*

167

later today. *Probably* first thing tomorrow, British time."

"But in the meantime Turner could warn Jackman. All he'd have to do is pick up the phone!"

"Right," said Wacko, nodding gloomily.

"Danny," said Joe, "you'd better get up to the hotel. From what you and Carlos heard the other day, lunchtime seems to be the regular time for Turner to call. Karen, you go with him. Try and check on all calls Jackman receives. Or, if he's out, hang around by the switchboard and see if one comes through for him. And what time they say to try again."

"But if he's inside his room when we get there and the door's closed—" Karen began.

"You'll know soon enough if he does get a warning. Mr. Jackman will be checking out fast. Now move! And the minute you hear anything of that kind, get back here quick."

Joe turned to Carlos.

"Ask Wacko to let them out of the house. Pronto! And tell him and Buzz that you and I will remain here until we do hear back. It looks like this will be our command post for the rest of the day."

Joe was wrong there, anyway. Before another hour had passed, Danny and Karen were back—yelling up from the yard and asking to be let in.

"Well, what's the news?" Joe asked, as soon as they entered the room, ushered in by Wacko.

"We—we got there just too late!" said Danny.

"Just too late to get inside the room, anyway," said Karen. "But we heard enough."

"You mean he *was* on the phone?"

"Yes," said Danny. "And another two minutes earlier, and I bet we coulda followed him in!"

"Unless he was *already* in," said Karen. "Before the call came through."

Joe nearly exploded.

"Never mind *that!*" he cried. "You've just said you heard *enough*. What *enough?*"

"Well, he was obviously talking to Turner," said Karen. "Because all at once Jackman started yelling too. He said, '*What?*'—like that. Then he said, 'But what *could* they find?' "

"Yeah!" said Danny. "And then I heard him say, not quite so loud, 'Well just keep cool, man!' "

Karen smiled.

"We could just picture Turner at the other end, dithering. And maybe Samantha clapping her hands."

"Sure, sure!" said Joe. "But then what?"

"Well, then it wasn't long before he came out of the room, studying some old yellow map," said Danny.

"The Sentinel Mountain area," said Karen. "I got a good look."

"Studying it even as he went out to the parking lot."

"Yes, but stopping on his way at the reception desk and asking them to have his bill ready for tomorrow morning. He said he was having to leave earlier than he'd expected."

"Good," said Carlos. "That gives Scotland Yard until tomorrow mor—"

"Not so fast!" Joe was looking worried. "If he was looking at the map, it means he was going to have one more try for the treasure. He'd know it would be his last chance, and he just couldn't pass up on it."

"Yeah—so?"

"So if he *does* find it this time, he'll be checking out right away. Today. There'll be no point in him waiting around a minute longer."

He turned to Buzz and Wacko, who were starting to look puzzled at the silence.

"Tell them, Carlos, right now, that we're all going up to Sentinel Pass—the whole squad, themselves included. We have to stick close to Jackman and see if he does get lucky. Then we have to think of a way to delay him somehow."

Carlos relayed the message. Buzz and Wacko turned from the screen.

"But how do we get there?" said Buzz. "We only have bikes. He's in a car. He could have had his last look, and struck pay dirt, and be long gone by the time we get up there. He must think he's pretty close to the hiding place by now."

"Yeah," said Wacko. "And it's too lonely up there trafficwise. We don't stand much chance of hitching a ride. If only *we* had a car and—"

He broke off. The green flicker of the screen had caught his eye. He turned. Buzz was already staring at the latest message:

"Taxi! Taxi! Taxi! Get a cab outside the station. And keep the doors open long enough for us to join you."

They reached the picnic tables at Sentinel Pond just after eleven-thirty that morning. They had got out of the cab a little farther down the hill, not wanting to give Jackman any warning of their arrival.

The cab driver looked at them as if they were crazy.

"There ain't no house *here*," he said.

"No, we're just out for the walk," said Buzz, paying him off while Wacko took his time emerging. "We get out here and walk all the way back."

"Good exercise," said Wacko.

"And downhill all the way," Buzz added solemnly.

"Kids!" grunted the driver, gunning his engine and making a contemptuous U-turn.

"I hope everyone had time to get out," said Wacko.

Four flicks on the right ear told him they had.

"Anyway, it looks like he hasn't found any treasure yet," said Buzz, when they rounded the bend in the road and saw Jackman's car, parked by the picnic tables.

Jackman himself wasn't anywhere in sight.

"He'll be over beyond the dead-tree place," Buzz continued. "Remember what Mike told us? He'd started on another tract—where the trees were still alive. We'd better approach cautiously, up the slope and along the rim of the—"

He stopped, suddenly getting the feeling they were alone, he and Wacko. Quite alone.

"You guys still with us?"

There was no answering flick of the ear. The four ghosts had heard enough. And, being ghosts, they didn't have to bother about being cautious in *their* approach.

Not with Jackman, anyway.

With Corporal Tom Bowes, it was a different matter.

"*Halt!*" he shouted, stepping from behind a tree, just as they were beginning to enter the wooded area beyond the blighted bowl. Already they could hear sounds of frantic chopping and digging. "Oh, 'tis you!" said the redcoat, shouldering his musket again. "Hast' come to . . . Jackman hard at work?"

Joe nodded. He felt uneasy. It wasn't so much the surprise they'd just been given, as the peculiar twist to the smile below that gap where the nose had been and a certain glint in the gray eyes. Maybe the Elemental wouldn't be so friendly toward them, back on his own territory.

"I see thy comrades have come an' all . . . Bezz and Wilko . . ."

Karen shuddered at this distortion of the boys' names. Like Joe, she was getting the feeling that the Tom Bowes who'd visited them in town was a different character from the Tom Bowes who ruled in this desolate place—a being to whom human speech counted for very little.

Buzz and Wacko were indeed only a few yards behind them now.

"Best tell them," said the redcoat, "tread most warily. . . . Master Jackman is getting desperate . . . and Master Jackman wields . . . a . . . like a butcher's meat axe."

Joe did what he could. Two quick clips on the left ear—two for each boy.

"What's that supposed to mean?" Wacko whispered, fingering where he'd felt the flicks.

"Probably a warning," murmured Buzz.

A flick on his right ear told him he'd been correct.

The ghosts moved forward, led by the redcoat.

"There! See thee?" he said, as they reached a sort of clearing, where the trees grew less closely together but the undergrowth was thick. "*Thy* Jackman! See how the swine sweats!"

It was in fact a machete the man was wielding—hacking at the undergrowth and pausing every few strokes to prod at the place he'd just thinned out.

"Just so long as he doesn't find what he's looking for!" said Danny.

"How so, lad?" asked the corporal. "What is it to thee? If he finds it . . . the lady . . . mother . . . surely safe."

Encouraged by this sign that the redcoat was still sympathetic toward them, Joe decided to explain.

So—while Jackman prodded and hacked and sweated and cursed, and Buzz and Wacko peered at him from behind a bush, well back—Joe gave their strange companion a brief account of Jackman's crimes in London and of how it was now only a matter of days, maybe hours, before the law caught up with him.

The corporal listened in silence, with bent head.

Not until Joe had finished did he speak.

"So," he said, "he murdered a man . . . a typical Jackman blow . . . from the rear. He caused the deaths of the lady in London . . . her children. That is known for sure? There is no mistake?"

Joe, Karen, Carlos and Danny all shook their heads.

The gray eyes smouldered—then blazed.

"Then by . . . he should be placed against . . . tree . . . and shot!"

Joe felt uneasy again.

"He—he'll get justice. He'll be taken to London and tried. Like I said."

"Aye! *If* the constables catch him . . . this great

distance . . . Bow Street! And him with the swift machine . . . and them . . . nobbut their horses? Art' in thy senses, lad?"

Joe sighed. He was beginning to see the real difficulty. Tom Bowes might have seen great changes around him over here, on his very infrequent trips to town, but he had no idea of what had been happening in his native land since the eighteenth century. Or at least only a very peculiar patchwork idea.

"Well, yes, Tom. I know what I'm saying. It *could* take a few days."

The soft answer seemed to calm the soldier.

"Then the runners must already be on their way. . . . But, my friends . . . Jackman will not remain here 'a few days.' Whether he finds the treasure . . . or no."

"No," Joe agreed. "But what can we do to detain him? That's what we have to figure out."

The redcoat drew himself erect. The smile returned. Cold, calculating, professional—more than a little cruel.

"For days? Thou'd have to cripple the bugger!"

"Cripple him?" gasped Karen. "We can't ask Buzz and Wacko to—"

"Overpower him then, lass!" The soldier turned his smile on the others and shook his head slightly, as if to say, "These squeamish women!"

"But we can't ask them to do that, either!" said Karen. "The man's a murderer. He's desperate. They could get killed. You said as much yourself."

The gray eyes rested on her. The smile lost some of its callousness.

174

Then the redcoat bowed, slightly.

"So . . . by your leave, miss . . . and since he is not *my* Jackman (for *that* one I should never spare) . . . *I* shall overpower him."

"You?" said Joe. "But you're a ghost. Like us."

"Ah, yes, lad. . . . But a very, very old one . . . with more than . . . two? . . . Aye, two centuries' experience. . . . I too have learned some craft. . . . I too have learned to speak with living beings."

"People?"

"Alas, no. . . . Not until I touched yon lads' ears t'other day. But—just watch . . ." He turned to the hacking, muttering figure of Jackman. "An't please you, I shall demonstrate. But . . . be sure . . . prevent the two young living lads . . . from coming nigh until . . . I have completed . . . *my* . . . communication."

They watched as he approached a clump of brambles, a few yards behind the toiling Jackman. The brambles grew around and over some large boulders. The gray stone could be glimpsed here and there between the leaves and tangled spiky stems.

The redcoat stooped lower, the closer he got to the clump. His right hand was extended, with the index finger and thumb making a circle—or, rather, a circle that was completed and fractionally broken so rapidly that it was difficult to see the movement of finger and thumb at all.

"What's he doing?" whispered Karen, as the redcoat's hand began to pass between the strands of briar, the circle still vibrating.

Then the figure of the Elemental stiffened, with the

hand still inside the clump, and he stood very still for about thirty seconds.

The leaves near his forearm began to stir.

He took a slow step back.

The stirring of the leaves seemed to follow his arm. His wrist reappeared as he took another slow step back, then the hand, then:

"Gosh!" Danny's eyes were popping. "A—a snake!"

"A *rattle*snake!" whispered Carlos, as the full dappled length of the creature, doubling and redoubling, slid into view, its head only an inch away from the vibrating finger and thumb.

They were soon in no doubt whatsoever as to the redcoat's intention. He was drawing the snake toward Jackman, who was now on his knees, prodding away, with his back to the advancing menace.

"He—he can't *do* it!" Joe's murmur was hoarse. "It'll *kill* Jackman! It—it's an *execution!*"

"Tom! *No!*" screamed Karen.

But it was too late. Her ghost scream became fused with the living scream of the man as he rolled on his back, kicking out and plucking at his right calf, where the snake had sunk its fangs.

"There," said the soldier, with the grimmest of smiles. "He is detained."

"But he'll *die!*" said Joe.

Buzz and Wacko were already running hard toward the writhing, moaning figure. The snake was already slithering back to its lair.

The soldier noted these things with what looked like no more than a mild interest.

"He will not die . . . if the two lads . . . act

quickly. . . . Take him in the carriage . . . to a chirurgeon or apothecary . . . in time."

Buzz was already kneeling over Jackman.

"I'm gonna—have—to take these off," he was saying, between tugs at the man's belt and jeans. "Hey, Wacko! Be careful. I'm pretty sure it was a rattler!"

"It was!" moaned the man. "It was! Please—help me!"

Wacko picked up the machete and was glaring wildly around him.

"Hey, you guys!" he muttered. "Do you see it? Has it gone?"

Carlos gave him a quick cuff on the right ear, and Wacko breathed more easily.

"How're you doing?" he asked, turning to Buzz.

"Fine, just fine!"

Buzz was sweating as he tightened the knotted belt a few inches above the already purpling flesh around the bite.

"Admirable!" murmured Corporal Bowes. "These lads . . . would have . . . splendid soldiers."

"You should never have done it!" said Karen.

"Lass!" said the corporal. "I could have directed yon . . . venomous beastie . . . to his throat. Then . . . even these . . . could not have saved him. But"—he shrugged—"he is *your* Jackman, not mine."

And with these words—which seemed to have become a refrain with him—he stalked off, back toward the bowl of dead trees and out of sight.

By now the two boys had Jackman, his face a ghastly greenish white, on a chair formed by their clasped arms, with his own arms draped around their necks.

"We're taking you to the car," Buzz was saying, in a gentle reassuring voice. "Are those the keys? In your shirt pocket?"

"Yes . . . oh . . . yes. . . . But . . . please . . ."

"Don't talk. You'll be just fine. OK, Wacko—let's go."

As they carried the swooning man to the car, Buzz said:

"Wacko—how good's *your* driving?"

"Not bad. I'm only waiting for my sixteenth birthday. Then I'll be all set for the test."

"OK. That settles it. You drive. I'll take care of him in back. I gotta make sure he keeps the leg down and be ready to shift the belt if the stuff spreads too fast."

Wacko just grunted. They had reached the car, and he was anxious to check if it was an automatic. It was. He sighed with relief.

"I mean I don't *think* anyone'll prosecute you for driving without a license," said Buzz, as he eased the now ominously silent man into a better position on the back seat. "Not in an emergency like this."

"They better not!" growled Wacko, inserting the ignition key and starting the motor.

The ghosts were already in the cargo area behind the back seat. Joe had been watching and listening intently. It obviously hadn't entered the head of either boy to hide behind any legal rights or wrongs and so neglect their duty to another human being—no matter how vile they knew that person was. It would have been so easy, after all, for them to leave Jackman to take his chances while they went in search of a passing car and a fully qualified and licensed driver.

And the others—they too were looking at Jackman with genuine concern.

"I hope they make it in time," said Karen, doubtfully.

"They will, if they don't get stopped by troopers on the way," said Carlos. "I mean those guys are always there when they're *not* needed!"

"In that case," said Danny, "if I was Wacko, I'd just let them chase me all the way to the hospital. I mean this is a matter of life and death!"

Joe couldn't help smiling. It was a proud smile. To him, the actions and comments of his young friends were so refreshing after all the talk of hate and vengeance he'd been hearing lately.

"It's what life and—uh—afterlife—are all about," he murmured, as Wacko swung the car into the road and floored the accelerator.

20
The Men from the Murder Squad

They did reach the hospital in time. They were neither stopped nor chased.

Jackman was very sick, though.

For the whole of one day, he lay in a coma, in the intensive care unit. For the next two days, he seemed unable to recognize his visitors. On the fourth day, he began to recover sufficiently to express uneasiness about his "business affairs," and a desire to get up and leave. He also demanded the use of a phone and was made even more uneasy by the fact that no one replied after several attempts to call the Hampstead store.

He was so uneasy, he got very nasty with Mrs. Green when she refused to smuggle in some outdoor clothes for him.

After she'd left in tears, he received a new visitor. Detective Officer Grogan of the local police department stopped by to say he was sure there'd been some mistake, but a man calling himself Richard Jackman had been passing a few bad checks in the area.

This caused Jackman to slump more than such a mild inquiry might otherwise have done. He'd been a crook all his life, and he knew the lead-up to a holding charge when he heard one. The local cops had obviously been detailed to keep an eye on him, pending more important developments.

And, sure enough, they developed.

The very next day, two large gentlemen came to see him. Their clothes might have been lightweight where they had come from, but they were much too heavy for a U.S. July. The men were grateful for the hospital air-conditioning.

They were accompanied by Grogan, a federal marshal and a man from the state's attorney's office. They were all very polite to one another, even to Jackman. There was one caution and a few brief questions, which Jackman refused to answer. But he slumped again and, instead of demanding to leave, tried to persuade the hospital staff that he was having a relapse.

The two visitors from England were very sympathetic. For much of the rest of the day, they sat with him as if he'd been their long-lost brother. True, the younger of the pair kept taking time off to chat and joke with the nurses. But the older never took his eyes off Jackman, except when the latter went to the bathroom—and even then he kept his ear close to the door.

And when Jackman left the hospital the following morning, the two Britishers were most considerate in helping him into the car that was scheduled to take them to the airport. One carried Jackman's overnight bag, and the other a bunch of magazines and newspapers to help the recent invalid while away the time on the long journey ahead. And their free hands were never far from his elbows, ready, it seemed, to steady him if he should stumble.

The four ghosts watched this touching departure. They too had been frequent visitors to the sickroom, though nobody had noticed them of course.

"Oddly enough," said Joe, "the dark-haired one mentioned Concorde earlier. He was telling a nurse that it was a pity the British Home Office couldn't spring for seats on it."

"Yeah, but Jackman didn't seem to care how long the journey was going to take," said Carlos.

"It's good riddance anyway," said Danny. "Whichever way they take him back."

"The tall blond one interested me most," said Karen. "When Grogan referred to him as Detective Sergeant Don Rose of the Scotland Yard Murder Squad, I nearly flipped. I thought, for a second or two, he'd said 'Tom Bowes.' "

Joe nodded.

"He was the one who never smiled—did you notice that? The other guy was saying that Rose had been on the case ever since the body was found in the quarry."

"Yes," said Karen impatiently, "but don't you see what I'm getting at? I mean it wasn't just his *name*. I mean take another look at him, before the car moves off. Those eyes. That mouth. . . . Just try to picture him without a *nose!*"

The others shrugged or shook their heads.

"Well, I *can!*" said Karen. "And—I mean—just think. Wouldn't it be something if he really was related to Tom? Maybe on his mother's side?"

Joe grinned.

"Come on, Karen! That would be too much to expect. And you know something? I'm beginning to think you took quite a shine to the corporal!"

Karen repressed a shudder.

"Maybe if he'd had a nose . . ."

"Anyway," said Joe, "they're on their way now. So let's go tell the others that that's the second of the two missions successfully accomplished."

The first had been announced to the whole world, the day after the showdown at Sentinel Pass. The following day's newspaper still lay on Wacko's table, near the word processor, folded at the page proclaiming the Ghost Squad's secret triumph.

TERRORIST BLOWS HIMSELF UP
OUTSIDE TEL AVIV HOTEL
3 Soldiers, 2 Policemen
Slightly Injured
"Lucky Escape"

"So that's that," said Buzz, when the news of Jackman's departure was relayed by Carlos through the word processor.

"Yeah!" said Wacko. "I bet those kids in London will be happy."

"I hope so," said Joe, to the other ghosts. "I wouldn't like to think of Samantha hanging around a couple of centuries and getting to be like Tom."

They were silent for a while.

Then Buzz said:

"Hey, you guys! What are you talking about? Share it—huh?"

"We were just discussing your summer help."

"Oh!" Buzz blushed. He'd been told about the redcoat by now. In great—and perhaps deliberately gruesome—detail. "Well, anyway—he *was* a help in the end."

"Sure was," said Wacko. "I wonder what'll become of *him?*"

The word processor screen flickered.

"Haven't you heard? Old soldiers like him, they just fa-a-ade away!"

Buzz perked up.

"Yes. But that reminds me. I'll tell you something that *never* just fades away."

"What?"

"The monthly phone bill! And you guys said you had an idea for supplying the squad with funds for expenses. You weren't talking of the Jackman treasure, by any chance?"

"No way!" Joe's message flashed across the screen. *"If there's any treasure still up there—repeat if—it wasn't where Jackman was looking. You can be sure of that. Because if he'd been that close to the spot, he'd be dead by now. Rattler bite to the throat—repeat—throat."*

"You think—?"

"Tom is the one who knows the exact location if anyone does. And that hoard is his bait—the only bait—to lure his Jackman."

"But *his* Jackman is a ghost," said Wacko. "Why would he want the money now?"

184

"The same reason he wanted it then, when he was alive. To gloat over it, of course. So if he ever did come back, it would be for the pleasure of gloating over it again—or at least gloating over its hiding place. But in our opinion even that wouldn't be strong enough to lure him. Not after two centuries."

"But Tom Bowes seems to think otherwise," said Wacko.

"He has to. It's his only hope of ever catching up with Seth Jackman. Anyway, what's more important is this: In the meantime, while he's waiting, Bowes will do everything in his power to keep that treasure from being discovered by living people, and being removed by them. And we know now that it really is in his power to do it."

"Snakes?" said Buzz.

"Yes. And if not snakes, other living creatures."

"Oh? But—"

"How about black widow spiders? Or fiddler spiders? (Fiddlers would be very appropriate, somehow.) Or even animals? A rabid skunk, say? Or rabid bats? We suspect that that guy has learned to lure them all."

Wacko gulped.

"So that *wasn't* your idea? . . . I hope!"

The word processor went straight into the reply.

"No! And this is my *idea, not Joe's or Karen's or Danny's, and you know what we do? We tip you off to the chances to earn some honest money."*

"Go on," said Buzz. "Tell us more, Carlos."

"Right. Well. We often see valuable articles that have been dropped and lost. Or pets that have strayed. With notices about rewards for finding them. Like, for instance, right now there's a lady's gold wristwatch lying in the grass behind a

rose bush at the edge of the Lakeview Hotel parking lot. We know for a fact there's a twenty-dollar reward for the finder."

Buzz and Wacko were already on their feet, grinning, their one last worry relieved.

"What," said Buzz, "are we waiting for?"

"What indeed?" said Wacko. "I mean, I don't mind the Ghost Squad being a nonprofit organization, but I'd sure hate to go bankrupt with it—no matter how good the cause!"